THIN ICE
AND OTHER
RISKS

STORIES BY

Gary Eller

Minnesota Voices Project Number 63

New Rivers Press 1994

Cover by Michelle Milne
Michelle Milne grew up in Apple Valley, Minnesota, and received her B. A. in
psychology and interpersonal communications from the University of Wisconsin-
Eau Claire. She has just completed a solo bike trip across North America.

The publication of *Thin Ice and Other Risks* has been made possible by generous
grants from the Dayton Hudson Foundation on behalf of Dayton's and Target
Stores, the Jerome Foundation, the Metropolitan Regional Arts Council (from
an appropriation by the Minnesota Legislature), the North Dakota Council on
the Arts, the South Dakota Arts Council, and the James R. Thorpe Foundation.

Additional support has been provided by the General Mills Foundation, Land
o' Lakes, Inc., Liberty State Bank, the McKnight Foundation, the Star Tribune/
Cowles Media Company, the Tennant Company Foundation, and the con-
tributing members of New Rivers Press. New Rivers Press is a member agency
of United Arts.

New Rivers Press books are distributed by

The Talman Company
131 Spring Street, Suite 201 E-N
New York NY 10012

Thin Ice and Other Risks has been manufactured in the United States of America
for New Rivers Press, 420 N. 5th Street/Suite 910, Minneapolis, MN 55401.
First Edition.

Acknowledgements

Grateful acknowledgement is made to the publications in which some of these stories previously appeared:

"The Habit of Despair" was published in *Stiller's Pond: New Fiction from the Upper Midwest* (Second Edition)

"Seeing a Cardinal" was published in a slightly different form under the name "Seeds" in *River City*

"Season for a Son" was published in *Fireside Companion*

"Thin Ice" was published in *Wellspring*

The author wishes also to express gratitude for the support and assistance of Connie Baron, Cheryl Latuner, Debra Marquart, Linda Morganstein, Steve Shuman, and especially, Hank Nuwer and Liz Carpenter . . . *Writers all.*

For Marianne.
Lover, friend, essential companion.

Contents

"In skating on thin ice our
safety is in our speed."

— Emerson

Thin Ice

I OPENED Sandra's Christmas present and wondered what I'd said that made her buy me skates. Figure skates, black vinyl with a flag emblem on the side. Made in the U.S.A. I tried one on for size. A little stars and stripes over my ankle bone waved me to my feet. I leaned on Sandra's shoulder, awkward and unbalanced.

This happens to me. I shoot my mouth about something, how it's smart, useful — or because I think it's an item I should like, and Sandra remembers. The next thing I know I own a fly rod or a five-year diary. Once it was a picture of a horse.

All my recollections of skating were unpleasant. Other kids played hockey, raced, cracked the whip and waltz-stepped with girls. I hugged the boards until my earlobes turned to crystal from frostbite.

That was long ago. Now I have a son twenty years old. I'd give him the skates, but he lives in Arizona and smokes.

I pulled into the park early. Winter's pink dawn cast lacy shadows through the trees. Only three people were on the ice, a woman and her two small children. In the warming house I wedged my feet into the skates, tugging the string through each eyelet, listening to the mother instructing her kids, her voice crisp as the January air. I stood. The soft splintered boards of the floor looked far away.

As I reached the ice more people arrived. A man with white hair curling beneath his stocking cap stood facing a woman. He walked backward in his blue tennis shoes, pulling the woman along. A drop of clear liquid on the end of his nose swayed with his movement. He passed the sleeve of his windbreaker over his face and a fresh drop formed, like the tip of a melting icicle. Across the frozen pond the kids sat flat on the ice, their short legs splayed, while their mother skated a slow circle around them.

The walkway ended at the edge of the ice. I heaved myself onto the surface. No friction existed between blades and ice, and my left ankle collapsed. They say not to fight a fall. I went down gently, like a schoolboy rolling in new snow, embracing the firmness of the ice. The man in the tennis shoes chugged past me, backward still, with the woman following, stiff-legged and wobbling.

Near the middle of the pond the mother turned, gliding on a single skate, and stopped near the ramp to speak to her children. Wisps of frosty breath marked her words. The kids followed her into the warming house.

I watched from our apartment as rain drops pounded the snow into dirty mushrooms. Sandra called from work. "Just wondering what you're doing," she said.

When she hung up I remembered the Winter Olympics and the finals of speed skating—the competitors in their bright aggressive nylon, thin and quick as whippets, devouring the ice ten yards at a stride. We'd watched together, Sandra and I, me cheering the Russians, Sandra for the Canadians and their maple leaf flag.

The weather turned. The pond's surface froze into a new arrangement of bumps and ridges. I studied the ice, searching for the smoothest places. When the mother paused also I asked her if she was from some polar locale like Minnesota. She was just from here, she said.

The white-haired man shuffled onto the ice, stopping here and there to poke a foot at a frost mound. "Everything's a matter of balance," he said.

At home Sandra asked how I was doing.

"Not too good," I said.

"But it's fun isn't it?"

Fun seemed like a quaint word, one that never quite fit the situation we were talking about. A word out-of-date, like double-bladed ice skates. It was a Sandra word. "I get good exercise," I said.

To strengthen my left ankle I rigged an elastic sling from the bathroom door. I began doing leg pulls, a hundred left, a hundred right. Soon the bumps no longer tripped me. I practiced until I could do parallel skid stops between two ridges. The cold air helped put a blush on the mother's cheek when she told me I was getting better.

Sandra worked next door to Wilson's and I'd asked her to check on skate sharpeners. She forgot, twice. I tried to let it go, then brought it up when she thought I'd gotten over it. She apologized. Then I apologized, but overdid it and she felt worse.

The union hall still offered nothing just right so I drove to Wilson's myself. A salesman with a terrible limp approached me, but rather than sell me a sharpener he carried on and on about how most problems beginners have result from a need for better skates.

When I got home Sandra had just hung up the phone. "That was Theodore," she said. "He could use you mornings for a couple weeks." She rubbed the inside of her hand on the side of her jeans, a gesture I always liked. "Starting the twentieth."

"Mornings are out," I said. "We agreed, right?"

"Agreed?"

"Yeah, I *thought* we agreed that I wouldn't take a job from a guy like Theodore. Mornings or nights."

Sandra shrugged and turned toward the kitchen. The refrigerator door opened, then closed. Sandra came out holding a stick of celery by its end, where the green broadens into white.

"He wants you to call him back," she said. The celery cracked.

My dad used to sit at the kitchen table using a tee to clean grass and dirt from the grooves of his golf clubs. "Maintenance," he said. "It's crucial. Take care of things or they won't be around long."

The inside whorl of the tip of the right index finger is most sensitive to touch. I ran it over the blade of the left skate and found a tiny rust spot, the size of a pore. Sandra reached to pluck a hair from my sleeve, blocking the light.

"Better tell him I can't make it," I said, working an emery board over the rust spot.

"So what do you mean—ever? Or just till the ice melts?"

"No, no," I said. "Just wait a little—until the timing is right."

"What is it that's bothering you?"

"It—you mean the timing?"

"No, I mean it—the *problem*." She rubbed her hand on her jeans.

"There is no problem," I said. "Conditions are just out of balance. And I think I need new skates."

Skates work by melting the ice under the blade—that provides the lubrication. The melted spot re-freezes immediately, but for a time, so short it can't be measured, there is liquid under the skater. I love to think of that. Floating on a long, thin river.

Christmas vacation passed and one morning the mother showed up alone at the pond. I wanted to offer her cocoa, but I'd brought just the one red cup.

Her name was Carolyn. Only about skating would she converse to any length. People think of figure eights, but there's much more to skating. Carolyn knew figure threes, mazurkas, dances like the Kilian and Choctaw, one and two foot spins, salchow jumps.

She was there the next day too, as I was trying to do circles. When I asked, she said my circles were pretty good, but that I was closing in, finishing too soon, forming sixes rather than zeroes.

Sandra got after me about the Visa again. I told her to make just the minimum payment. She said it's twenty percent interest. I said what are credit cards for? She said to just forget it.

We went to a movie, arrived late, and got seats in the front where we sat watching Tom Cruise against rows of windmills turning in a hazy background. Sandra stayed home the next day. When I got back from the pond she lay asleep on the couch, her head on her hands, the orange afghan wrapped around her.

Sometimes we do things wrong our whole lives. Carolyn showed me how to tie my skates. They should be loose at the bottom, she said, then tight through the instep with a surgeon's knot, and loose again near the top. I studied her skates. GOLDEYE, they said on the sides. She told me the boots were double insulated, made from imported French leather.

Wilson's said to try Chicago. I made four calls before finding someone who heard of them. The man I reached seemed to think he should shout.

He said he didn't stock them, but could place a special order. They start at two hundred dollars. They were top of the line, he said, for serious skaters. So good the skater just goes along for the ride.

"Goldeye blades are *German* steel, temperature-hardened," he said, barking the word "German." I thanked him.

It rained again. I thought about offering Theodore two mornings a week. Sandra and I watched an old "Hill Street Blues." Renko's wife was deceiving him. The weather turned colder.

I waited until Sandra left for work before getting up. I threw on English Leather, made cocoa with a little less sugar, and remembered the extra cup.

When Carolyn got there I was on the ice, practicing threes, conscious of the drag on my blades. She stepped down the ramp, her white scarf around her shoulders. Starting on the far edge I made a curving glide toward her. The resistance eased as I sailed past. I backed, turned, and followed her frosty breaths.

We sipped cocoa in the warming house. The redness of her cheeks softened as she smiled. We talked of cinnamon toast and oatmeal with raisins, and speculated about the rubbery skin that formed on cold cocoa. My English Leather mixed with the odor of oil and pine from the floor. Heated air shimmered above the little stove in the corner.

Carolyn had skated every winter since she was eleven, including the two she'd been pregnant. Before the babies, she came to the pond alone. Her husband was from Tennessee and hated ice. He hated the whole northern part of the world, Carolyn said, but teaching jobs were hard to find.

"Do lots of people skate during the day?" Sandra asked.

"Not many. Why?"

"Just wondering, you know, if people had to go to their jobs or whatever."

The phone bill lay on the table, the Chicago numbers circled and checked. Sandra looked at me.

"I really love you," she said.

Carolyn began bringing treats, trail mix and fig bars, to go with the cocoa. I asked her to show me how to position for a jump. She took my hand, and my mitten slipped off. I reached for her, bare-handed. She flipped the mitten in the air, smiled and spun away.

On Valentine's Day I brought her a tiny wax-paper package containing a sugar cookie shaped like a heart. She tasted the tip, re-wrapped it and tucked it in her coat pocket. She skated around the pond, leading with her weak shoulder, stretching with each stride, the cookie safe in her pocket, the white scarf dancing behind her.

I skated too long, and came home tired. Sandra had fixed barbecued ribs with corn and fried potatoes. She kept the dinner warm in aluminum pans covered with embroidered dish towels. She watched me as I ate, then handed me a box wrapped in red tissue.

"Open," she said, rubbing her hand on her jeans.

I wiped my fingers, balancing the package on my lap with my elbows. I tore the tissue away and read the lettering on the box: GOLDEYE.

I worked the heel of my hand into the side of a boot, smelling the husky richness of the leather. I ran my finger down a creased blade. Its flat side caught the white light and skipped it back to the ceiling.

"How did you know?" I asked. She blinked and shrugged.

"Happy Valentine's," she said.

On a corner of the ice where the surface froze in a polish I imagined I could see myself, gliding on one skate, my back arched, my knees bent, the trailing blade in the air, my hands tucked out of sight. When I stopped, a shower of shavings exploded from the surface and floated away in my wake.

Once, many months ago, I drove through the park on my day off and saw Carolyn, balanced on a single skate, carving long slow circles in the ice. By then it was nearly spring. The air carried the rich aroma of moss along with the hum of the ice across the pond. I waved, but Carolyn didn't see me.

The white-haired man has disappeared, and Carolyn has moved to Virginia. Alone on the ice now, I turn on a notched blade and scull backward, slowly at first. Two sets of tiny thread-like tracks from the hollow ground blades follow me, leaving a spiral trail. My arms follow the line of my body in a natural curve. One foot crosses over the other, the air parts and makes way before me. I might be standing still. I'm skating.

Independence Day

IN MEMORY OF A FRIEND

"BAD NEWS," said Darryl. And he told me.

We were climbing the wooden steps to Bulldog Bandstand, located that winter in the Eastern Star Hall, a charming stucco building demolished in the seventies to make room for a physical fitness center—a project that followed the wheat farms into ruin.

"I heard it on CKY," Darryl said, over his shoulder. "An airplane crash in Iowa."

Diane Truitt sat stamping hands with a rubber marker, the album next to her ink pad. "You heard then," I said to her. She nodded, not looking at me. Other kids bunched up behind us, drawing quick last puffs from the cigarettes in their cupped hands.

Darryl pulled his sleeve up so the ink wouldn't show. "Right there," he said.

I waited in the backwash of his cologne, envying that excellent hair while he checked his watch and adjusted his belt, bending the moment to his style. He swung the tall door open. "Let's dance hard while we're still alive," he said. Light, heat, and the hard, confident sounds of "Peggy Sue" spread into the night and drew us in.

Elvis looked like the guys who steal socket wrenches from shop, but with those glasses and the tie Buddy Holly looked like a scholar, like a boy stepping out of chorus recital to sing a tenor solo. Parents loved him on the album covers.

We knew the difference though, and expected music to wither when

7

Buddy Holly burned up in that airplane. The stations at the low-number end of the dial would go back to the songs of Patti Page and Vaughn Monroe, the music of the war generation, of our civics teacher Stengler.

Stengler insisted our vile rock-and-roll would destroy us the way smallpox wiped out the Indians. He lined up every entity in the world, past and future, with its natural agent of demise. Corrupt royalty finished Europe. Communism couldn't survive because it sprang from Mongols. South America was backward, and Africa lacked motivation—the inhabitants preferring to sit around picking sores on their feet while waiting for foreign aid. "Be glad from the bottoms of your hearts you live in the U.S.A.," he said.

Stengler was as far from caring if we learned about Dred Scott as a frog is from Emily Dickinson. He could tell us anything—we didn't object, as long as it demanded no action. Those who disturbed him were at the ends—like Howard Steinmetzen, who got out of fourth grade when his knees hit the bottom of the biggest desk. And Darryl Willkie—curious, unafraid to disagree, and armed with a disturbing and logical memory.

Darryl represented what teachers claim they want in youth, but despise when they get it. "Then why are Communists still legal?" asked Darryl. Stengler walked his chalk around his fingers and cracked it with his thumb. "Your lawmakers have no guts. That's why."

For four years, starting in sixth grade, Darryl and I shared everything— Popsicles and funny books, then cigarettes and copies of *True*. We called the movie the *show* and took the same seats at Eden Theater—third row, first two from the left.

Darryl had the build of a farmboy, but lacked the weary farmer's gait. His was the limber step of an athlete. My sister Katie adored his Sal Mineo eyelashes. Mother liked him for his manners. Dad paid little attention until Darryl made two mistakes: He quit the basketball team, and got a car.

Farmers could sign permits allowing their children to drive at fifteen. Darryl came up with an ancient Packard coupe, ignoring the many Plymouths and Chevys available. It had shiny floor pedals, heavy doors slanting out at the top, and smoky cloth upholstery that billowed dust when you slammed the door.

We left the dance and headed the Packard toward the river. At Wayne's U-Drive-By where they sold three-two beer to anyone tall enough to slide money across the counter Darryl paid for two quarts of Schlitz and a cigar with an ivory tip. We rode up Main to the square where the brick road fronted the gazebo. We got out, carrying our quarts by the neck, and went up the steps, side by side.

"And Ritchie Valens, too," I said. "Bad stuff's happening to kids."

Darryl poured beer into a wooden stein. "Were you there when Stengler talked about when Glenn Miller got killed?"

"Who Miller?"

"You know. Glasses and trombone. They say his orchestra affected people's morals."

That struck me as hilarious. "An *orchestra?* "

Darryl scratched a wooden match on the side of the step, bathing his face in orange. "Yes, in Stengler's day sex probably needed encouragement."

Wally Morton's pickup rolled by, bouncing over the brick road, the bed loaded with fence posts. I waggled my finger at his tail lights.

"Look at that dumb ass," I said. "Thinks he'll get girls into his cowshitty-smelling pickup." I swallowed air and offered a loud beer belch to the night. "I'm sick of this place. I can't wait to get out."

Darryl's eyes glowed as he tasted his beer. A distant, idiotic laugh came from the direction of the fairgrounds. He rested his elbows on the step behind us and let his head fall back, studying the sky, his throat a triangle of white. He'd heard me say that a million times.

And just as often, I'd heard him defend the town. "We're lucky," he said. "My cousin in Elgin misses the place."

"What's to miss?"

Darryl blew smoke toward the sky. "Who knows? Maybe it's our famous river flowing north." For some reason Darryl thought that was remarkable, the Red River going the wrong way.

The curfew siren blew. Sarge was playing cribbage in the pool hall. Kids didn't bother him — so long as they stayed away from Dakota Street where the mayor lived. The siren ground to silence. My imagination was jumping. The Schlitz tingled in my nose. I said, "Why *did* you quit the team?"

Darryl knocked the ash from his cigar. "Basketball's not that important."

"Geez," I said. "What's more important?"

He didn't answer. He studied the grooves on his beer stein, humming softly. Appreciating the moment—that's what Darryl did best. In the sky over Canada the northern lights flared, deep and measureless, climbing and falling. His voice took on that older tone again, like someone home from college. "You really want to know?"

I hesitated, fearful of some moral lesson. Lately Darryl took everything so serious. He stared into the patterned darkness of the sky. The tip of his cigar brightened and faded like a distant warning light. "*Time*," he said. "What's time mean to Buddy Holly?"

I became an intimate of my own car—a bulky, hundred-dollar Ford with a fickle reverse gear—bought on a whim with birthday money from my grandpa. Dad groused around, but finally reasoned that I wouldn't run with Darryl if I had my own transportation. Darryl was different, he said.

Usually after practice I'd ride with a teammate past the square to the fairgrounds, thumping the wheel to the beat of the radio. We'd meet Darryl in the Packard and offer a wave that was no more than the twitch of a fingertip. Occasionally a girl appeared with him, her hands gesturing as she talked—sometimes a certain type of girl, like Joyce Hoaglund who pretended it didn't matter if you showed up at her back door.

"It doesn't figure," I told Rodney Burdick. We'd parked by the gazebo, passing my last Marlboro back and forth.

"Les, are you dumb or just stupid?" Rodney said. He blew smoke through his nostrils without inhaling. "Watch in cafeteria how he sits. They got codes and secret mannerisms. Pull on their ear lobe. Scratch their ass with their little finger. Stuff like that. Just watch."

Joyce pulled me close, her cheek forming the hard curve of a forced smile. "Someone told me I'd have to make the first move with you," she said.

Larry McBride had prodded me to dance with Joyce. We two-stepped through a Platters song and she was ready to leave. *Just get her in the car, Leslie*, Larry said. *She'll do anything.*

We kissed. She levered herself upright with an elbow and spit a wad of gum into her palm. "You better have brought a rubber," she said.

On the main highway cars passed, their snow tires whining. I leaned toward her. "We can be careful."

She tapped a fingernail on the front of the dashboard. "I won't do it without." She twisted the rearview mirror, pulling at the corners of her mouth. She had all the power in the world. "I thought you all carried Trojans, the way you talk," she said, folding her arms and moving her feet together. "Now I'll never find out."

Her knee cracked faintly. Her allure was fading. I started the car.

"Boy, you give up easy," she said. "Maybe it's true."

My neck was stiff from turning. "What's true?"

Her reedy voice bounced through her words. "They say Darryl Willkie's a homosexual."

"Who says?"

"All the kids. It's all over school."

"So what's that got to do with me—you think I'm queer or something?"

She waved a hand in contempt, as if anyone who went around Trojan-less deserved no further judgment. "You guys were such *pals*. You'd know if it was so."

"Why don't you tell *me*?" I said. "I've seen you with him."

She drew a sharp breath. "What are you accusing me of?"

"Forget it," I said. I let the clutch out and pulled onto the highway, the Ford swaying on its weary springs.

We drove in silence past the Dairy Queen outside town. Joyce produced a tissue from somewhere and blew her nose loudly. "Mr. Stengler says they should lock up homos and throw away the key."

Later that year Darryl's Packard was gone, sold to a dentist who collected antiques. I'd see Darryl, eyes down, broad arms swinging, with a preoccupied step that said he was doing fine, hiking by choice.

I gave him a ride to school once. Rain fell in sheets and my broken wiper made an unnerving screech on the glass. Darryl ran his hand over my new seat covers, and said the radio sounded made for Buddy Holly. When my reverse gear jammed in the parking lot, Darryl said the problem might be in the transfer case. "I can show you how to pull it apart," he said. I thanked him and told him I'd let him know.

"Have you had a tiff with Darryl?" my mother asked.

"Tiff?" Dad said. "Good Christ! What are they, cats and dogs?"

"Darryl's a nice boy. I don't want Leslie falling into the wrong crowd."

"Maybe *Darryl* is the wrong crowd," Dad said.

Katie's annoying voice called from the kitchen. "*Dad*-dy. Maybe Leslie's the wrong crowd."

Wally Morton told the boys at our lab table that Eugene Krenz saw Darryl with an erection in the locker room after gym.

Chuck Johnson looked at me, then at Wally. "Sure, and Stengler got caught in the Rose Garden with Jackie Kennedy."

Wally was short and bushy-haired, with a morose face that lied easily. "No, honest. Why do you think he undresses in the stall?"

"Come on," I said.

"You're sticking up for him then?" said Wally.

"Wise up."

"The hell you're not. Coach Hedlund says he'd of made all-state, so why'd he quit?"

"You're crazy. He hates practice is all."

"Yeah, but he loves the shower room, right? Who knows, Leslie, probably you'll be the *next* one quitting."

The Ag Club voted to gather signatures on a petition demanding the candidates clarify their positions on price supports. Darryl and I were paired to man a card table outside his uncle's realty office.

Most offices closed Saturdays. We watched the shadows of people advance through the foggy, chicken-wire glass of the outside double-doors. Many citizens had already signed at the Super Valu. Others didn't understand what we were doing, but happily wrote their names where we pointed. Sam Graber asked us who we supported. Darryl said Kennedy. I said Nixon.

We sat there until mid-afternoon, listening to Darryl's portable radio, twisting the silver antenna. I counted the names. "Fifty-two. That's enough," I said. Darryl hesitated but said nothing. We were supposed to stay until six.

I carried chairs while Darryl unlocked the office door. Striped ribbons and medals with cast iron rifles hung on one wall. His uncle was a war hero. On his desk rested a pistol-shaped cigarette lighter. A long sword mounted behind the desk caught my eye.

"Is that an army saber?"

Darryl took it down. "A samurai sword," he said. His finger traced the etchings on the handle: square-sailed boats, houses with swooping roofs, and strange pictographs. "Such beauty. Imagine. Don't you love old things?"

I didn't, and said so. "There's too much new I need first."

Darryl looked at me hard. "You know Les, I bet you can't name me three things you'd really like."

I faked a laugh. "Are you crazy?"

"Three things you're without. Only they have to be reasonable. You can't say a million dollars—nothing like that. Reasonable."

I thought a minute.

"Go ahead," Darryl urged.

"Okay. To make state in basketball."

Darryl pursed his lips. "All right," he said. "And?"

"To go all the way with Diane Truitt."

Darryl shrugged. "That's two."

"Then. Well." The reasonable part made it rough. "I'm not sure," I said after a long silence. "How about you?"

Darryl lowered the sword, pointing it at the floor. "Nothing," he said. "At least nothing that makes sense to me."

I wanted to leave. This was Darryl from the third row at Eden Theater, the jaw more angular now, and the voice deeper, but I didn't know him anymore. The sword frightened me. The dark stains on the blade made me think of blood.

He tapped the tip on the point of a star woven into the carpet. "Les, why did nobody understand when I quit basketball?"

I felt momentarily better—basketball, I knew. I reminded him the Bulldogs hadn't made it out of districts since the war. "You'd average twenty a game easy, Darryl."

"You're saying *you* understand?"

"Yes," I said, lying. "You need time."

Darryl fell into his own thoughts for a minute. "But it's not the same," he said.

"What isn't?"

His cheeks reddened. "As with you."

The air felt heavy in the little office. The walls reeked of ancient plaster and smoke from a million cigarettes. "I'm not following," I said. That also wasn't true. What *was* true was that Darryl was different. My dad was right.

"I notice Diane too," he said. "I love her in that red skirt." He arched his eyebrows like Groucho Marx, but the brightness faded immediately. "The thing is, what's friendship mean?"

"I don't know," I said. How could I answer that? "It's when you like being around somebody."

A shadow moved across the outer doors. Darryl gave a start, coming to life. "We better go."

Outside on the steps, I felt I could breathe for the first time all afternoon. Darryl turned to me. His eyes were so large and full of feeling they seemed about to leave his head. "I appreciate you standing up for me," he said.

I wasn't aware I had stood up for him, but I nodded. Down the street Rodney Burdick came out of the pool hall, wearing his brother's purple and gold letterman's jacket.

"You know Les, I never thought I'd get so lonely," Darryl said. "Do you think we could go back to the way it was before, when I had the Packard?"

I remembered the first time he took me for a ride, recalling our joy at mobility and independence. "Sure Darryl," I said. "Why not?"

We took Government II together the next semester. Stengler was energized now by the new president's plans to turn the country over to the Russians, and still trying to figure what regulation the school board might turn up to use against students too smart for their own pants.

"You kids. With what's going on you ought to worry about something other than that so-called music that's got your brains so addled." He scanned our faces. "Howard. Sit up straight and tell us what the Bill of Rights is."

Howard squinted into his blank notebook. "It's where they tell about voting."

Stengler fingered his chalk, surprised that Howard's wild guess made a connection. "Voting. What else?"

Rodney covered his mouth and kicked Howard under the desk. Stengler ignored him. "Diane. What say you?"

"Isn't that the first section of the constitution?"

Stengler nodded. "We're getting closer. Darryl Willkie, you're conspicuously silent for once."

Darryl brushed his hair back. "I know the most important part of it," he said.

Stengler nodded. "Well please share it."

Directly behind Darryl, Eugene Krenz snorted and grabbed himself in the crotch. He looked so goofy-faced I burst out with a laugh. Darryl glanced at me. "The idea is citizens can do anything they want as long as they don't hurt anybody—even if they're born stupid as Eugene."

Eugene cupped his hands and barked into Darryl's back, but Darryl didn't even twitch.

Stengler hitched his pants, glaring. "Well, that's not precisely so."

"Yes," said Darryl. "It is exactly."

"And how are you so certain?" asked Stengler, shuffling papers on his desk.

Darryl's head hardly moved as he spoke. "I've read it many times," he said. "All four hundred and seventy-five words."

The gazebo smelled of paint. The grass was freshly mowed, the red brick street swept clean. Herman Greenup rode the fire department's cherry-picker, stringing striped bunting from light poles for the Fourth of July parade.

A few of the guys gathered around the square: The two Larrys—McBride and Ferguson, Wally Morton, Rodney Burdick whose dad just got a job selling GMCs, Chuck Johnson who was three weeks away from a tryout with the Baltimore Orioles, and Darryl—stranded in town waiting for parts for a broken binder.

We were sticking to the shade, drinking Cokes from the new pop-top cans. Drinking and burping. Passing the time, applauding our youth. *It's probably a hundred thirty in Dallas Texas. How do you know? I been there. Your ass. Yours too. Stick it. You stick it. Is that Dorothy Hansen on the bike? Nah, I can tell by the knockers.*

The heat was layered and substantial, lying thick on every surface. Roofers on the drugstore moved their rollers around, working the tar. On the ground the diesel engine on the melting tank putt-putted in the summer sun, overpowering all but the beat of the song from the Ford's radio.

"What a shit job," said Rodney.

Chuck lay stretched out on the grass with his T-shirt rolled up. Twin
rows of blond hairs led down his belly. "Might have picked a cooler day
seems like," he said.

"*Hey,*" said Wally. "A hundred Swedes went through the weeds, all chased
by one Norwegian." He danced past Chuck and grabbed my baseball cap,
yanking hair at the same time. Grandpa had mailed me that cap from Bloom-
ington. Wally flipped it to Rodney who scrambled over the hood to the roof
of the Ford where he stood beating his chest, like Tarzan on a hippopotamus.

"Get down before you dent it," I said. Rodney threw the cap to Darryl
who inspected it, brushed something from the crown, and handed it to
Wally who looped it to the roof of the gazebo.

With a foot on the railing and my fingers dug into gunky dead leaves
I pulled my chin even with the rain gutter. A wasp whined past my ear.
I grabbed the cap and leaped into the soft dirt of the flower bed. Wally
offered his hand as if to pull me out, but instead snatched the cap and
tossed it back up to the roof. Once more I climbed to retrieve it.

Wally pounced on my can of Coke and raised it to his mouth. His
throat worked as he swallowed.

"Bastard," I said.

He crunched the empty in his hands, set it on the ground and stomped
it with his foot. "Your ass," he said, sweat rolling off his red face. When
he grabbed the cap again I caught his T-shirt, stretching it as he pulled away.

"All right you two," said Darryl, his voice soft.

But Wally wanted more of his stupid game, holding the cap out of my
reach as he worked loose. I could see it, the white logo smudged, the bill
bent. I bunched my hand into a fist. Darryl stepped between us, the smell
of deodorant faint on his blue shirt. "Just hold it," he said.

I wanted to crunch Wally's ugly nose. I tried twisting free, but Darryl's
strong arms were locked around my chest. I kicked at his shins. "Goddamn it, let go of me you *fairy,*" I said.

Darryl's hands dropped at once, his face forming a picture of wide-eyed
astonishment. Then came the surprise—he grabbed me by the shoulders
and flung me toward the Ford like I was a bale of hay. I landed in the
rough turf edging the sidewalk, tumbling, shredding the skin on my knee.

Somebody—one of the Larrys—yelled, "C'mon you guys."

I meant to bounce right up but couldn't get my footing. The disconcerting feel of the hostile hands lingered on my shoulders. Bits of bark and grass stuck to the back of my neck. A shadow appeared and I looked up. Darryl stood above me, his hand extended, dark and calloused. Heat bubbled up from the bricks. I rolled away.

Wally dropped the cap on the ground, his eyes glistening with excitement. The thump of the diesel sounded through the warm air and echoed off the buildings behind us. Darryl walked past me without a word, his head erect, his face as vacant as the blue of the high summer sky.

I got up, brushed off my pants and concentrated on picking dirt from the meaty part of my hand. I craned my neck around. "Is my shirt torn in the back?" I asked. Nobody answered.

Chuck snatched a ladybug off a dandelion, pressed it in his palm, then released it. He turned to Rodney, "Hey shit-for-brains, go get me a Coke."

"Your ass," said Rodney. "Your royal ass."

In the last clipping I have of Darryl, he's shaking hands with Indira Gandhi. Neither of them looks healthy. Mrs. Gandhi has deep rings around her eyes. Darryl's head is bowed, his dark hair thinner. It looked hot wherever they were—Mother had trimmed off the caption.

The land in Darryl's family was spacious with rich soil, more than enough to support Darryl and his brother. But Darryl wasn't interested. While I sold twelve-string guitars in the store across from the gazebo, Darryl was teaching Pakistani peasants how to read directions on seed packets, studying earthen dams, and reading Thomas Merton. He married a woman from Pakistan, a doctor, as I understood. The marriage lasted about as long as my own.

The summer of Nixon's second election I spent in my old room, watching Viola Johnson's clothes flapping on the line across the fence, trying to get my bearings. Dad had died. The music store folded. Mother was moving to Stockton to be close to Katie and the girls. The phone rang the night of the Fourth. It was Larry McBride.

"Hey!" he said. "Come on down, we're celebrating."

"Celebrating what?"

"The war's over. Kissinger says so."

"Did you hear I'm still off the booze?"

"The Vendome sells orange juice last I heard. Seriously, Les. Know who's here? Darryl Willkie."

"Darryl's in town?"

"Pulling out tomorrow and he'd like to say hello. Can you make it?"

"I don't know. Last time I wound up in detox. What's going on with Darryl?"

Larry spoke above the hammering jukebox. "The same. He's all over the world but says he's gonna settle down in California. Listen Les, just order your Coca-Cola and forget it."

I pictured the two of them at the table by the door. Larry with his emerging pot belly. Darryl with his soft eyes and worldly manner, nodding gently as Larry recounted small stories of life in the home town. It sounded pleasant. "Does he know about me?"

"What's to know? He says he hasn't seen you in ten years. Now are you coming or not?"

"I can't," I said. "My mother's sick. Just tell him hello."

After Mother moved away she maintained a steady stream of delicate letters, assuring me I sounded great, congratulating me when I found work, sending small checks when I didn't. I kept her supplied with clippings from the Star: Chuck Johnson made it to double A. The Bulldogs were state runners-up the year Nixon quit. Diane Truitt bought two Hallmark shops in Bismarck. And Stengler died the very day Hinckley shot Reagan – for all I know done in by the grim news.

Mother phoned infrequently, like the rest of her Depression-era generation. When she did, she offered news in a careful voice. "You'll never guess who we found out lives in Stockton. *Darryl.*"

I knew that, from Larry, but I pretended surprise.

"Now finally you'll *have* to come visit," said Mother.

"Maybe," I said. "Tell him hello."

"Oh, I never see him," she said. "Katie read it in the newspaper. He's been in India doing *wonderful* work."

Grandpa died the following January, and now Darryl was home for his own dad's funeral. The layers of generations were thinning above us.

He approached the car from my side, those strong wrists slender now.

New Rivers Press
420 North 5th Street / #910
Minneapolis, MN 55401

New Rivers Press, a non-profit literary
publisher, began in the winter of 1968
with the idea of publishing the work of
new and emerging poets. And while lots
has changed in the world since 1968, our
commitment to publishing the very best
new writing has not. In addition to poetry,
New Rivers Press also publishes collec-
tions of short fiction, essays, translations,
and anthologies. New Rivers Press books
are available at fine bookstores, or directly
from us. To receive our free catalog and
learn more about New Rivers Press, please
fill out and return this card.

Name _____

Street _____

City _____

State _____ Zip _____

I lowered the volume on the tape deck and we spoke. I told him I was sorry about his dad. He knew Mother lived near him in Stockton, and was surprised to hear she was in town. To keep the conversation going until Mother finished in the post office, I told him about my bad back and asked him how his health was. He shifted his feet, bracing himself against the car door. "I'm dying, Les," he said.

Mother appeared with a bundle of envelopes rolled up in a magazine. She put a hand on the fender to step off the tall curb, and Darryl hurried to help her. Someone honked and someone else flipped her blinker on to claim my parking spot. Darryl waved me away with a thump of his hand on the hood. How do you pack twenty years into five minutes?

But that evening we spotted him entering the Vendome. He almost ran down a woman leaving—but stepped back, made a grand gesture with his arm and bowed, as if he were welcoming Mrs. Lars Jensen into the Taj Mahal instead of the Vendome Bar. "Go ahead and go on home," I said to Mother. "I'll be along."

I felt nervous about entering the place—the scene of so many of my troubles—as well as about seeing Darryl. I came up behind him. "Got time for an old friend?"

He turned slowly, smiling. "Sure do."

We sat. Stella set out napkins for Darryl's gimlet and my Coke. "I hear you're getting back on your feet, Les," he said. "I'm pleased."

I thanked him, and mentioned all the second chances the agency had given me, and how grateful I was. "I might even get married again," I said, and told him about my girlfriend Denise.

I finished my Coke, too quickly. I'd carried our meeting that far and wasn't sure where to take it next. Darryl came to the rescue. The old soft eyes looked vacant and tired now, but the self-assurance and instinct for the deep was still there. "They have this drug. It's experimental." He hesitated, as if searching for something. "This place needs a little music," he said.

"The drug, it helps?" I asked, as if instead of just beginning, we'd proceeded far into a discussion.

Darryl gazed across the room, looking the way he did back in Stengler's classes when he knew the answer, but didn't want to come out and say it. He spoke a single awful word: *Prolong.*

Stella came by and took my glass. "Want another?" she asked.

"Maybe this time I'll have rum with it," I said.

Darryl looked up sharply. "Don't do that," he said.

I didn't really want a drink. I said, "It's just hard to take, news of a good friend."

Darryl brushed his thinning hair back. I still liked that tiny vanity of his—he hated getting his hair messed up. "Les," he said. "We weren't that good of friends."

In her last letter Mother added a dispassionate paragraph advising that Darryl had died. I've cried over matters easier to solve than death. But I put the letter in a drawer with Christmas cards, photos of Katie's kids at the lake, and clippings with the familiar saw-toothed mark of Mother's pinking shears—material piled up over the years, much with no reference point, just facts floating around looking for a reason to be.

Mother was still living in Stockton about the time Darryl got sicker. I imagined him lying there losing weight and helpless against every piddly germ that came along, surrounded by condominiums and irrigated green peppers—alone as a falling star. I remained here—I never really wanted to leave—getting better, studying for my realtor's license, helping Denise's son with his jump shot.

Now the tug of memory is so faint and fading that the town has become friendlier than I recall. I seldom think of Darryl for I realize I only comprehended him in relation to myself. I'm changing. He'll always be the same.

But I do remember how we sat side by side on a winter night with our feet stuck out and our hands in our coat pockets. The gazebo in the square is still here. Our winters are very cold. The Red River flows north to Canada.

Waiting for Extinction

SONYA ASKED to hold the newest Crudup baby — a puny-armed boy, fresh and warm. Alice Crudup handed him over, his head pitching and rolling on a sorry neck. Sonya nuzzled the red face, breathing the delicate powder, and passed him on to Collins who lay the infant against his lapel and tapped two fingers on his tiny back. The baby stretched, burped, and vomited down Collins's leather jacket. "It's all right," said Alice Crudup. "Company upsets him."

At home, Sonya draped the jacket on a wooden chair, spraying foam from a blue metal container over the stain. "I wonder what we'd do with a baby," she said, speaking through a steady aerosol hiss.

Collins knelt on the kitchen floor, the *Sporting News* spread before him. He groaned, shifting his weight to turn the page. "I guess there aren't that many options."

The refrigerator kicked in. Sonya looked up. "What was that?"

"Nothing I think."

"No, I heard a brassy noise — like a clock."

Collins walked on his knees to the refrigerator and pulled the door open. Glass jars rattled. Cool light flushed his face. "Where'd that piece of cheesecake go?"

The Collins house displayed its aging personality with great, audible complaints. The garbage disposal screeched, light bulbs crackled in their sockets, shingles scratched and fluttered.

"If I could avoid the streets I'd bike to work more often," said Collins, in bed. "Save on the car and pedal off some of these pounds."

Sonya rested a hand on her abdomen, rolling toward Collins and blocking his reading light. "What's your opinion on a three-month trial? No sponges, no foil, no estrogen from the urine of horses."

They'd had it before, this conversation, and the situation was beyond settling, capable of resolution only by the fact of a baby—in which case someone would be unhappy. Collins cleared his throat. "If this is a poll, put me as undecided."

The roof gave a shuddering, hollow moan. "What's *that?*" said Sonya.
"What's what?"
"How could you *not* hear it?"
"It's wind in the soffits," said Collins, yawning.

Sonya persisted. "What do you think? Let's decide before my folks get here. I feel like I push against life and it doesn't push back. Isn't it important someone be sad when we die?"

Collins rested his newspaper on his belly. "The night my father died I drove eight hundred miles, and when I got there my mother and sister were shopping for a coat, and my brother-in-law was watching Roller Derby on TV." With a grand effort he rolled over. "It's a matter of priorities. Things aren't going so good at work."

While Collins seemed uneasy around children, Sonya saw babies in the conventional way. She longed for a shadow of her own face—nostrils less severe perhaps, but a breathing entity, fingers and toes, the stored energy of a whole new human. She thought of her ova as clusters of grapes. *Eggs*, her mother called them, from a diminishing number, dropping and drying. Sonya was thirty-six now, and each passing month saw another unmolested egg wither, shielded by changes in acidity, isolated behind a wall of latex like a bubble baby.

Sonya used two pot holders to carry the spaghetti to the table. Steam condensed on her glasses and wet her forehead. Upstairs, something made its presence known—a loose, clattering item in the wall, like a forgotten chisel attempting escape. Collins looked up from the floor, elbows on his newspaper, beer at his side. "I'm starving," he said.

It pleased Sonya that her husband was known for his eating style. When

Collins reached for his fork no conversation was necessary or possible. He was a serious eater. Even the neighbor dog Rascal took no interest in Collins's discarded pork chop bones. Two years earlier at his thirtieth birthday party he ate half of his chocolate cake in one sitting.

Sonya waited as he blotted up the last sesame seed with his little finger. "My mother says if people waited for a reason to have babies the race would become extinct," she said.

Collins looked satiated and content. "Is that necessarily bad?"

Feathers of frost were forming on the window. Outside, Sam Crudup was using a snow shovel to shape a pile of leaves. "It's seems like a reasonable requirement, to replace the two of us—like our parents did."

"I was the third kid," said Collins.

Collins was an actuarial systems analyst. Not only did Sonya wish he'd become something self-defining like a tree surgeon so she wouldn't have to explain his occupation, she was convinced the work made him analytical. "You *know* what I mean," she said.

Unlike most men, who sought confrontation, Collins had a way of defusing tension. "That reminds me. What day do your parents get in?"

From the garage came a screech like a rhinoceros sharpening its tusk with an emery board. "Thursday. If we could tell them we're planning a baby it would be wonderful."

"Oh boy, I need the car Thursday," said Collins. "Can Alice run you out to pick them up?"

Sonya nodded, not really listening. She lifted a soggy tea bag from a saucer, dangling it by the tag at the end of the string. When they first married she sent away to St. Louis for bulk teas and tungsten mesh infusers in three sizes. The merchandise arrived UPS, delighting them with a rich Oriental fragrance through the sturdy packaging. Now she drank Lipton's, plain, heated in a microwave.

"Some people say children represent a duty," said Sonya.

"Don't we have a duty to each other?"

Sonya heard distinctly the noise of adhesive tape being ripped off skin. "I'm not sure we'll even stay together without more in our lives," she said.

Collins blinked. "Don't say that!"

"But somebody has to preserve the race. What's supposed to keep a man and woman together?"

"Love?" said Collins. "Please, honey, let me get past this pressure cooker at work, okay? The job is killing me."

Sonya leaned forward in her chair. "That's what I mean. Having a child will save me. And then I'll save you."

In high school Sonya was deliciously promiscuous, following lovers into back seats of Olds Cutlasses, Super Beetles, girl scout tents — nestling upright in broom closets, the odor of Spic 'N Span brisk in the cramped air. An assortment of oily boys rolled out prophylactics by night but were disinclined to lock eyes with her in the honest light of fluorescent cafeterias — never speculating that fifteen years later she'd continue thrilling them with effervescent memories.

She'd met Collins at the laying of the cornerstone for a new Arby's. Two indifferent mall grazers, star-crossed by commerce. Sonya could never get over it. She'd gone shopping only as a favor to an ill friend whose son was desperate for an ant farm. Little things make our fate.

Collins with his passion for thrills had wandered over, drawn by the crowd, anticipating distress — a portly man respiring profoundly, a thief in chains. Instead he found complimentary RC in tiny paper cups, spread out to warm in the sun. He gathered two and leaned against a nearby car. Sonya's car.

In the park next day they walked far into the woods, plucking mulberries that Sonya carried in her outstretched skirt. Collins brought a blanket, a paint-splotched radio, a thermos of Stash tea. "I'll never get the stains out," Sonya said later, shaking her skirt.

She barely controlled her urge to tell him everything about herself — that she voted for Reagan to provoke her friends, that she adored TV talk shows, and that she was at that moment pregnant by some jerk. Which jerk, she couldn't be certain. She loved Collins because he seemed infinitely needful. She wanted to nurse, chew, and smother him. She wanted to pour sugar over his body and squeeze him to a sweet, tenderized pulp.

"Why do you look so dejected?" she asked him when they reached the car. "Are you tired?"

"I always look sad when I'm happy," he said.

They married in a month. Collins found a better job, Sonya had her abortion secretly, and they moved their scant belongings into the ancient, two-story frame house next door to the burgeoning Crudup clan.

Collins rode helmeted and toe-clipped down the driveway and past the cluster of mailboxes, flexing steely calves, his briefcase strapped to the fender. Sonya watched, noting the portions of his buttocks enclosing the saddle seat. She'd always thought she'd never love anybody fat, but there he was.

He rolled past the Crudups, wobbling up the incline, and pedaled through the stop sign just as something bore down on him from the left. He swerved. It veered, honking, squealing—a mad mass of blue Tokyo metal.

In a moment too soon for gladness, Collins appeared simply puzzled to be alive. He balanced the Schwinn between his legs, both feet on the ground, as if noticing mostly the still-sticky asphalt, laid down last week by a yawing yellow machine. His crotch rested gently on the bar. He turned, waved, and pedaled on. All was well.

Sonya stood on the sidewalk, marveling. Later she'd recall that she relished this pre-shock phase, confirming that references and advice are all about us, waiting for interpretation.

A Crudup boy appeared on the porch, looked at nothing, and slammed the door on Bryant Gumbel's adolescent voice, in extreme depression, apparently, over the day's prospects in his public education.

Sonya waved at him. "Hi Zachary," she called.

"I'm Skylar," the boy answered.

In the house Sonya hugged herself, rubbing away goose pimples. Images and unfinished idea fragments wedged themselves like weevils into her consciousness: Yogi Bear's face on a night light, bibs with strata displaying the three basic food groups. Bottles by the dozen. Band-Aids by the gross. Entire landfills stuffed with Pampers.

She located her purse, rummaged through it, and dropped her pills in the garbage can. The dishwasher sighed. Mr. Coffee hissed. Sonya was out of Tampax.

They sat on the front step, Collins with his bag of cheesy potato chips, Sonya with tea, watching Sam Crudup and his sons throw a football. The ball came boinking toward them, bouncing crazily, and stopped at Sonya's feet. Collins wiped his hand on his pants, and without leaving the step, heaved the ball high over the crab apple tree into Sam's waiting arms.

"*Hey*—Joe Montana," yelled Sam.

"Did you play sports? You never told me," said Sonya.

"Oh, there's lots you don't know," said Collins, returning to his chips.

Sonya thought that over, wondering if he meant to open up a hole for conversation. "Would you like a son?"

Collins spewed crumbs making an answer that sounded like *Don't know*, but may have been *Nope*. Sonya thought he preferred daughters. He barely tolerated the Crudup boys. When forced to converse with them he'd ask about cowboys or other items from his own childhood about which they showed no visible interest. "Daddy would like a boy. I never made him very proud."

Collins wiped his mouth. "Well, not on the football field," he said.

"Not for *anything*," said Sonya. "I wonder what it's like. No one *ever* applauded me."

She realized Collins was right. There was much she didn't know about him. That must come from marrying so quickly. They had no gestation period, no practice maneuvering resulting from a long engagement. With no opportunity to stake out territory and test feelings, their histories became buried. *Maybe forever*, she thought.

Back inside, away from the boisterous Crudup games Sonya folded her arms, steeling herself. "Are you having an affair?"

Collins looked up from the floor, his mouth forming a frightened oval. "Of all the things. No, and why do you ask?"

Sonya wasn't relieved. "Once or twice when I call they say you left the office for the day. Only you don't come home early."

"When does this happen? You know how Dottie garbles things."

"Last Thursday for one."

"I made an agent call Thursday, yes."

"And our money. It makes me wonder when Mother asks if we plan to *ever* get out of this house."

As if in protest, the noise of canvas ripping sounded from upstairs. Collins ignored it. "I see," he said. "Somebody's put a bug in your ear."

"Not at all," said Sonya. "You know my folks think the world of you. Our car's falling apart. Every month we get calls. You never wanted me to work. Why aren't we doing better?"

"Honey, we will. Just wait."

Sonya had a thought. "Good Lord, it's not cocaine, is it?"

Collins smiled wearily. "Not unless Reese's is putting it in the peanut butter cups."

"I'm sorry," said Sonya. "But you're so distracted. Is it the idea of a baby?"

Collins lowered his ample chin. "It must be my job. But I do wonder, what if you liked a baby more than me?"

Sonya's mother worshiped melancholy. Her respiration consisted of endless imperfectly punctuated sighs. She loved to lament generations unborn and spoke constantly of going to her grave without this or that, as if her grave were a place that already existed, like a muffler shop. "If only God would send a little miracle," she said, over and over.

All four attended mass, joining their huddling neighbors in devout parallel lines. The church was warm, its spacious interior a sturdy comfort against the rain knocking the last tan leaves from the boulevard oaks. A young girl, precious, dark eyed, dressed in white, was receiving her First Communion. Sonya watched as she took the wafer in her hand, closed her eyes and placed it on her tongue, considering. So God was dry and tasted like paste.

"Wasn't she adorable?" Sonya said, speaking over the gasp of the drain pipe from its weekly Comet purge. "I liked the young priest. Let's join that parish."

Collins lunged for Sonya's wrist. "I prefer a more earthly devotion."

Sonya shrieked and covered her mouth. "The folks!"

Collins pulled the drape aside, looking to the right, then to the left. He made a moustache of his index fingers and rolled his eyes crazily. "Zey are *pree*-soners of zee Crudups."

Sonya followed her husband to the bedroom, happy, astounded. In her memory, men seldom wanted her more than two or three times. Or was it the other way around?

"Just imagine," she said, after they'd made love. "Thousands of sperm chasing a single egg."

"Like the Green Mill on a Friday night," said Collins, kissing her forehead. "Anyway, tell that egg she better stay well-hidden for a while yet, okay?"

Collins hinted that he expected his father-in-law to attend to the grumblings of the house that had been bothering Sonya. But he was no help, leaving

Collins looking disappointed that an elder was as baffled by tools as he. The older man, hard of hearing and still wearing his Colts cap though his team was long departed, kept cocking his head comically as if imitating Sonya, saying, "What's that gosh-awful noise?"

Nonetheless, Sonya knew Collins welcomed her parents. They contented themselves with television and in admiring the Crudup children. They caused Sonya to prepare astounding dishes in their honor, and they took her on vigorous shopping excursions, returning with Uncle Sam marching dolls and quart jars of macadamia nuts. Always, after a visit, they mailed fat envelopes bearing five dollars postage, stuffed with ads for jobs near the Chesapeake Bay.

The old folks delivered an invitation at the moment of parting, their boarding passes ready, Sonya in tears. "Come to Baltimore," her father said, winking at Collins. "You all work too hard up here. We'll get you on the right track."

Collins stood over the sink, spooning ice cream from a half-gallon carton. By the gruesome way he contorted his knuckles to probe the corners, scraping out the last lumpy spoonful of pink sweetness must have been the most important thing in the world to him.

Even as she watched, Sonya found she couldn't stop talking. She was exploding with ideas. She spoke of a recipe for sweet potato pie, of the reason women eat plasterboard, the origins of beanbag furniture, and how sailors tell where they are. "I think there's a great shield out there," she said. "Everything we do bounces back, like waves, pushing and pulling at the same time."

She hadn't been so cheerful since her parents left, and she guessed Collins let her wander on, not wanting to ruin all her spilling conversation. "How do you like that?" he said. "The milk freezes and the ice cream melts."

Sonya counted on her fingers. Granted, eight days wasn't much. This did not *necessarily* mean a pregnancy. Those things were confusing, those days overdue. How did they count again? No matter. It felt just like the warm blossoming of the first time.

Collins worked his spoon quietly as if thinking. Sonya walked behind him and laid her head between his shoulder blades. Did he know? She reached around and hugged him, pinning his arms. He pulled his stomach in.

"I've been jabbering so much," she said. "How was your day?"

His weight shifted on his hips. A joint cracked. "You don't want to know."

Sonya loosened her grip. "Of course I do."

Over his shoulder Collins said, "I got fired."

Outside, Zachary or Skylar was peeing on the frozen ground beneath the crab apple tree. Sonya watched. Something large but light-weight took off from the roof. She walked back to the table, trying to erase the waddle she imagined she'd suddenly developed, and sat down heavily. The Crudup boy was shaking, tucking, zipping. "Fired from your job?"

Now it was Collins's turn to pour out words. "It's not all bad. They'll give me a recommendation for when they open up in Billings. I'd be first in line. The thing is, I think I got it worked out. With unemployment and if you could go back to Benny's and pull in some dollars we could just make the house payment. We'll seal up the spare room. No extravagances. Dinner at home, and then if we got a U-Haul."

"Billings Montana?"

Collins still held his ice cream carton, looking confused, as if fearful that carrying it across the room to the fridge would seem frivolous. "Right, the trouble is, my medical expires in thirty days, and Billings won't open till June so we're looking at a good seven months of risk." He tried a little joke. "You know how us actuaries are about risk."

"Let's get out of this house—I hate it anyway. Those awful noises."

"Remember we talked about that? The market's way down."

Sonya sniffed several times and wiped her eyes with her wrist. She circled the string from a tea bag around her index finger. The end of her finger turned red, then purple. "Why'd they fire you? You work so hard."

Collins's earnest gaze fell to the floor between his feet. He spoke softly. "Who knows?" A small group—a woodwind quintet—passed through the laundry room heating duct. Collins moved toward the table, carrying his wilted and dripping ice cream container. "Do you think you could manage that—going back to Benny's? I know it's difficult, on your feet, selling."

"It was your idea I quit, remember?" Sonya blew her nose into a dish towel. "Don't step in your mess." She blew her nose again. "First, I'd like to go to Baltimore for a while. Do you mind?"

"Oh, honey. I don't know—without a Super Saver. Do you realize how broke we are?"

Sonya could see, actually *see*, snow flakes filtering through the curtains, hear the flakes blowing across the kitchen table, and feel them settling around her heart.

"I need the car tomorrow," she said.

"I guess I can take the bike," said Collins. "It doesn't much matter if I get there late just to clean out my desk."

"We need to talk more, don't we," said Collins, that night, from his side of the bed.

Sonya rolled on her back. "Maybe."

"But isn't it strange? All the couples we've known who hug each other so much, like love birds. They hold hands in the grocery store, then next thing you know they move away and get a divorce."

"Strange," said Sonya.

Collins put an arm on Sonya's shoulder. "We're going to get closer from talking," he said. "I promise. Tonight was just a start."

"Closer," said Sonya.

Sonya lay awake, thinking. Maybe the baby was defective—she'd set herself up for maternal disaster. All those sweeteners. Pot, hash, chamomile tea. Ravages from the audacity of youth. She envisioned her chromosomes, hideous revolting things, frazzled wire-like fragments barely making contact, genes loose in their settings. Birthmarks, crooked spines, ears that don't hear. Disease. She tugged on her waistband. Her panties were too tight.

When still she couldn't sleep she tiptoed down the hall to the spare bedroom, lay across the floor on a diagonal and wrapped her arms about herself. That felt better. She pulled her knees to her chin, rocking. A sob rose from deep beneath her stomach where her mother used to say emotions are born. Acid tears washed over her cheek in rivulets and stained the powder blue carpet while the furnace wheezed and moaned.

The Emma Goldman building looked the same, but now something was happening. Beefy policemen mumbled into radios. Women in berets and long coats shouted to passing cars. Sonya drove on and circled the block, skipping Euclid to avoid the cathedral. A squirrel ran onto the street. Sonya braked, watched it cross, and continued.

She told herself she'd go around the block once more and if still she couldn't find a parking place it meant she wasn't supposed to be there. She wondered what her father had said when he learned her mother was pregnant.

She circled the block twice, meeting cars with well-dressed couples riding in the front and back seats, the way they do for funerals. On the second pass a white van pulled out of a space. Sonya pulled in, feeling ashamed to allow a trivial matter determine the fate of a life. Her mother would say let God decide. She sighed and checked her bag for Kleenex.

Uneasy people moved about with hand-lettered signs stapled to sticks. A teen-age girl, all hair and panache, denim-jacketed against the cold, hissed at Sonya. "*Mommy!*"

The unexpected single word, hurled so inappropriately like a dart, stopped Sonya. "What?"

"I love you," said the girl, her voice softened in apparent surprise at having gotten a response.

"Are you crazy?" said Sonya.

At once several others formed a semi-circle around Sonya, eager for confrontation, waiting on the margin of an event. "Do you love me?" asked the girl, as a cop approached to warn the people back.

"Can I go in?" Sonya asked.

"If you have a good reason."

The cop was small, narrow-hipped, younger than Sonya, a doubtful bulwark against the awfulness of society. He carried the appearance of somebody's last child—unplanned perhaps, but a receiver of his own First Communion.

"Tell me," Sonya said. "Have you ever made a mistake?"

"Pardon me?" The cop spoke to Sonya but kept his eyes on the protesters.

"A mistake," said Sonya. "What happens when you're wrong?"

"Ma'am, if you're not sure what you're doing here you should talk it over with your husband or boyfriend or whatever." His expression didn't change. He must say this all the time. "Now are you going in, or not? I have to keep the way cleared."

Sonya turned away. Behind her, the little band of protestors rested their flimsy signs in the crooks of their arms and spanked their gloved hands together, applauding.

Sonya waited at her favorite place, the kitchen table, poking restlessly at the lemon wedge in her tea and checking the window. Orange streetlights blinked and came to life. Inside the Crudup house on a long couch sat the matriarch Alice, the curve of her forehead and her crescent mouth duplicated, triplicated, quadruplicated in the chain of happy blond heads beside her—all grinning at their flickering blue television.

A square of soft yellow light covered the driveway where Sonya had left the garage door open. Collins's broad shadow crossed the concrete. He was home. The garage door closed. The yellow light vanished.

Collins hung his helmet on the hook next to the kitchen door, ran a glass of water and sat down across the table from Sonya.

She looked at his glass. "Not even a beer before dinner?"

He patted his midsection. "Fat."

Sonya attempted a smile.

"Look," said Collins, taking a deep breath. "I've been thinking all day about our talk. There's something I need to tell you about."

Sonya stiffened. "Me too."

Collins shifted uncomfortably, scooting his chair closer. "Mine goes way back," he said. "It's a situation I didn't handle well. Before you came along I got involved with someone and she ended up pregnant."

Sonya stared, unblinking. "Pregnant. Who?"

Collins shook his head. "I couldn't—she married somebody else. I've been giving her money, for years now."

Collins went on, detailing his various concerns—the house payment, the old student loan, the furtive visits to the little daughter in Ames and his fear of being discovered. He spoke for ten minutes, the words cascading. "They told me I was taking unauthorized time off. Then they found out I'd been borrowing from one of my accounts."

Sonya pulled a tissue from the box on the table, trying to picture a child of Collins. Nothing appeared. "If only I'd known."

Collins attempted a clumsy hug across the kitchen table. "A baby, what could I do? They're moving too. I can end the payments."

Sonya nodded, studying her husband. He ought to somehow look less troubled for having unburdened himself so. "Maybe you shouldn't," she said. She realized now why she still loved him. His requirements went on and on.

"Mother called. She's sending a ticket as an early Christmas present. She offered two—if you're interested. Are you—I hope?"

Collins walked heavily to the window, staring into the cool November darkness. "I thought you were going to tell me you were leaving for good," he said, dabbing his eyes on his sleeve.

Sonya caressed her stomach, tensing it to build her confidence when something interrupted her—a harmonious musical hum, like fine wire set to singing by a warm breeze. Gathering her thoughts anew, she spoke.

"Actually, there's more to tell," she said. "Much more."

The humming faded, but Sonya could tell by the astonished expression on his face that Collins had heard it also. For a long moment the two looked at the ceiling and then at each other, waiting and listening—as if whatever happened next depended on nothing more complicated than sound.

A Hundred Reasons

A THUNDERHEAD rolled over the hill from the west, pushing fat and warm raindrops that struck the newly laid shingles on the treehouse with satisfying slaps. Potter sat under the peaked roof, snug and secure, engulfed in the sweet aroma of pine. With his thumbnail he scraped a bead of tar from the inside of the door jamb.

Cyn stepped through the brush, surprising Potter. She held a piece of Visqueen over her head. "Are you up there?" she called. "I'm leaving for work. You better get some sleep."

"How's it look?"

"Fine," she said, turning. "Try not to wake me when you get up, okay?"

Before he started lugging cross beams, boards, nails, tar, insulation, hinges, tools, and a ladder up the hill to build his treehouse, Potter understood that the most remarkable thing about himself was that his resident girlfriend and both of his wives all had the same name: Cynthia—though only the first wife used the full name.

Co-workers in the bakery, salesmen, customers—all rolled that fact over in their minds, trying to connect it to a theory that might explain such an aberration. They'd say it must mean *something*—though they couldn't determine just what. But Potter saw the name as just a word—hanging on three individuals as different as the sun, the moon, and Mars.

The treehouse represented a diversion that somehow got out of hand. It started with a chunk of two-by-six on a stump—a place in the shade to rest and watch for hawks after a steep climb. Potter realized the view would be spectacular if the bench were elevated, so he dragged several four-by-fours up the hill, one at a time, and fastened them with U-bolts to the broadest limbs of a bur oak. The resulting platform surprised him with its sturdiness. It felt so solid and well-built it demanded a roof and walls.

During the intense building over the summer—scaling the ladder, stretching the tape measure, driving nails—Potter began earning the fulfillment he once found only at the bakery in the years before automation, when the immense toil provided him an almost blessed satisfaction. The treehouse gave him something more to think about, crowding out unhappy notions pointed at his home life and at his future with Olafson Bakery.

The project also became an item he could talk about with Cyn—one noncontroversial enough to avoid ending with a slammed door or wounded silence. Cyn kept up interest adequate to get a sense of the treehouse's appearance—the diminished dimensions, the chalet-style roof, the snug Dutch door. "Why's it so small?" she asked.

Potter couldn't say. He wasn't thinking of the result, only the process. He knew that it would accommodate a single person, one not too tall. And by the time he nudged the last window in its frame he found he'd become so accustomed to ducking and dividing by two that the world had become too big. He continued bobbing his head as he passed under arches, and curling his feet beneath his body when he sat. He strained to look over steering wheels. Overstuffed chairs seemed like immense, inflated bags. He came to dislike open spaces. He decided that the best dimension for any room was a little less than seven feet.

As he sat in the treehouse, knowing it was invisible from the trailer house as well as the road, he felt secure, beyond trouble's reach. When finally he'd attached the last shingle, latched the door and hauled his tools down the hill, the sensation stirred him that at last he'd found a place he truly belonged.

Potter ladled four measures of regular grind Maxwell House into the metal basket and filled the tank with cold water to the line on the side. He waited, listening for the rumbling and sputter. When the first of the morning crowd slipped in the side door they'd find coffee bubbling and hot.

In a sense Potter was responsible for the bakery serving as a coffee shop. Bluto and Granger had started dropping by at the end of night shift to eat Potter's strudel and pecan Danish. They brought others: three or four shop owners, the dentist, the lawyer Dick Charleton. These were people, all men, turning the corners of their day, sliding through the dimension between work and home, cashing in their claims on the community— reward and responsibility, a privilege Potter hoped to share some day.

Bluto and Granger entered from the back, walking stiff-legged from hours in the squad car. "Just the man we wanted to see," said Bluto. "We got complaints from out your way." Bluto's shirt tail hung over his unbuckled holster.

"Complaints?" Potter said, sliding tan mugs across the counter. "What kind?"

"Proutys and Kovacs claim somebody's been in their storage sheds." Bluto set his big teeth into a caramel roll. "It's kids."

Ben, the jeweler, turned sideways in his booth. "They're all on dope," he said.

Gene Granger squeezed behind Potter in the tight aisle, searching for coffee creamer. "We'll make a couple extra circles out that way with your lady by herself and all," he said.

Isaac Olafson liked the idea of his bakery serving as headquarters for the town leaders. He put in a longer counter, tacked up colored posters of pastries seldom seen among his wares, and hauled in three booths and a table, purchased cheap from the drug store when the owner tore out his old soda fountain. Olafson took the tall booths the way they were, with nail holes and thirty years of carved initials still visible.

Olafson had told Potter the business would be his some day. Already Olafson spent winters in Scottsdale, and said he was looking at desert property, waiting for his daughter to finish school. Dick Charleton, from his booth by the door, cautioned Potter often. "Do you have this in writing actually?"

It *was* worrisome to Potter when Holsum ran a truck up out of Devils Lake. But Olafson's product was good and the customers knew the difference, knew that Olafson Bakery turned out fresh bread right here in the old hometown. Potter built his own reputation for the fine pastries he prepared. He told himself that when Olafson did sell to him, everyone would know why he stayed so long, and understand that he was a lot smarter than they'd thought.

"So what about it Potter?" Bluto said. "Seen any kids on the prowl — probably you get a good look at them from your *tree*house." He snorted, spewing crumbs on the counter.

"Shut up, Bluto," Granger said.

"Potter, you got a gun just in case?" Bluto pulled out his service revolver and laid it, muzzle to the window, on the Formica counter. "For sure he can shoot, hah Geno?"

"Put that away," said Potter.

Again, Ben's wheezy voice climbed the partition. "You fellas ought to shoot the town. Then *every*body can go to Devils Lake to buy watches."

Potter longed for the comfort of his treehouse. He stared out the window where the Olafson delivery van, painted to resemble a loaf of bread, sat parked next to the squad car. "Hey you guys, you leave a prisoner out in the car — what if one of the councilmen comes in?"

Bluto wiped his mouth with a paper napkin. "It's just Jake. Give me the dice. We'll shake to see who takes him over."

The dice clattered on the counter. Bluto frowned. "Damn," he said, thumbing donut into his mouth.

Granger waited until his partner left. "Potter, loosen up."

Potter took Bluto's seat, toweling the counter as he sat. "One of these times he's gonna get hurt waving his gun around like that."

Granger brushed his long hair back from his eyes. "Nah, you know him, charmed life. What is it, you fighting with your lady again?"

"Bluto makes me jumpy. Gets me thinking is all."

Granger leaned back, jingling the change in his pockets. "Ease off. You got it made. A place in the woods and a real fox to come home to."

Potter lowered his voice. "To tell the truth, things aren't so great with Cyn."

"I knew it. Cops got a sense for trouble."

"Sometimes I'd like to dump everything and pull out."

"Potter, you go through this every six months. I wish you were serious. I'd buy your place right now." Granger raised himself so he could see through the window. "Which reminds me, they froze the overtime, but if you want I'll lean on Bluto for what he owes you."

"Let him be," said Potter, examining his calluses. "I haven't got around to cashing last month's paycheck yet."

When Bluto and Granger were ten years old, and Potter nine, Potter had tagged along when the older boys took their .22 rifles to the gravel pit for target practice. On the way Bluto shot at everything he saw, gulls overhead, meadowlarks on fence posts, insulators on telephone poles. When he offered to let Potter try the rifle, Potter shook his head.

"What are you, pussy or something?" Bluto said. "I knew we shouldn't of let you come with."

Potter took the gun. It felt lighter than he expected. A jackrabbit bounded from the ditch. Potter fired. The powdery pop of the rifle and the screech of the rabbit as it tumbled and rolled made noises Potter heard for years afterward. He stood rooted to the gravel path, trembling. The brown bundle twitched in the grass. Potter imagined the glob of lead, hot and heavy, searing the intestines.

"Look," Bluto said, standing over the rabbit. "You got him in the asshole."

Potter turned away, tears stinging his cheeks. "Jesus, you guys," Granger said. He placed his foot on the thin front legs of the rabbit, held the muzzle of his own gun against the creature's head, and fired.

Bluto broke the dense silence. "Good way to shoot your toe off, dummy."

It was Granger who'd called, then drove to pick up Potter when the first Cynthia had the accident. On the way to the hospital Granger slowed so Potter could have a look. Ernie Tisdale already had his wrecker backed up to the car, and Potter would remember that he wished he could save the tow fee since it appeared you could get behind the wheel, gun it, and roll right through the ridge of snow and back on the highway. Home in time for supper.

"See—just a bumper's banged up from the culvert," said Granger. "There wasn't a mark on her. She was walking around, talking to the paramedic."

"Doesn't that sound like Cynthia?" Potter said. "Organizing her own evacuation."

At the hospital, still wearing his paper baker's hat, Potter met Sister Mary Jerome coming through the double doors.

"Is she okay?" asked Potter.

The nun nodded slightly, choosing her words. "She's not conscious just now." She motioned the men to the side. She'd been at the wedding, sitting near the front with the other nuns. "She took a jolt."

Behind him, Potter heard the scratch of Granger's Bic. Sister Mary Jerome looked past Potter. "Please take your cigarette to the lobby."

"Then she's having an operation, or what?"

The new doctor—the one whose wife played tennis—pushed through the doors. "I'm sorry, she's gone," he said.

Gone? There wasn't a mark on her. Father Bournier came through the lobby, walking softly, nodding to the right and left, his robe brushing plastic chairs. More than one person was talking.

She's *dead.* Died.

You said gone.

She lost consciousness.

I saw the car.

Gone?

There wasn't a mark on her.

You know, when it's internal.

There wasn't a mark on her.

Doris Ryser offered to sing. Something from the Carpenters, she said.

You bastard, Potter said to himself, even as Doris sang, even as necktied men braced against the weight of the straps. Pallbearers—an old, hollow-sounding kind of word. Standing on the green carpet by the hole in the ground, Rondecker's Lincoln hearse with its maroon skin shined to heavenly elegance. *You bastard,* because even now he couldn't get his eyes or his thoughts away from the alive Cindy Riggs whose manner gave off a sadness far deeper than Potter could make himself feel.

Olafson told Potter to take as long as he wanted. Potter came back the day after the funeral. Classmates, friends of Cynthia, girls she'd been cheerleader with expressed surprise to one another at seeing Potter lining up loaves of Russian rye for the bagging machine, checking his watch, peering over the top of the oven door, mumbling to himself.

The same ones dropped by the apartment carrying covered plates with ridges separating roast beef, potatoes, and string beans to reheat. This went on for a month. Then they all forgot about bringing meals to Potter. All except fair-haired Cindy Riggs.

"You don't have to talk yourself into thinking you loved her, just because she's dead." They sat in Potter's car outside the bakery where Cindy had waited for him.

"This is a beautiful hardship," she said, the first time she saw the wooded five acres with the big hill in back. She told Potter she saw nothing wrong with spending the insurance money on it. A trailer house and septic tank would be fine with her.

Cindy Riggs was in those days taken up with causes: the plight of Tibetans, eradication of the dingo in Australia, freedom for Zambia, Lithuania, Nicaragua. "Please understand," she said. "Please."

Mail came to her daily from this or that committee. She seemed in constant examination of suffering. Potter considered it an odd notion, getting that involved with distant, invisible unhappinesses. He liked to think he anchored his love close by, in the good he wanted for her.

"Wouldn't it be wonderful raising a child out here?" he told her as they walked the woods.

"No — unless the rest of the world changes," Cindy said.

Other times she talked about her own child, wishing aloud she'd kept the baby. Potter wanted kids and a savings account. Cindy Riggs told him he was callous and selfish. He asked her, didn't she think she was naive? She saw him as small-minded and provincial. Off he'd go to work, eager for the noise, the routine and the satisfaction of repetitiveness extended to pain.

When they were juniors the band traveled to St. Paul for the Winter Carnival. Cindy Riggs wanted to ride a city bus over to Minneapolis, insisting she knew her way around. None of the other girls were willing to leave the hotel at night. Cindy went by herself, ending up at the bus stop near Como Park where a group of boys called to her, then approached. Friendly at first, something stirred them. Cindy was attacked, raped, her mouth held shut by a gloved hand that smelled of gasoline. Four boys — one wearing a sweatshirt with a W on the front — it was over in twenty minutes. The Twin City Federal thermometer read twelve degrees. Most of her sixteen years Cindy had been hearing of the dire things that could happen to girls who weren't careful, or who thought the wrong things, or sent questionable signals. Now, in the gloomy winter veil of a big city, it had happened to her in twenty minutes.

Cindy returned to the hotel and stood in the shower for forty-five minutes, convinced she was pregnant. She put all her clothes on and went to bed. No position felt right. She promised herself she'd make up for her mistake by entering a convent. She decided if she could cry it would help. She concentrated on *Old Yeller*. But the harder she tried, the closer she came to laughing until finally she did laugh, out loud, waking her roommate. The roommate ran for their chaperone, Mrs. Winkler. By the time the desk clerk called the police no one was left in Como Park.

A few weeks later Cindy Riggs missed her second period. For her parents, Cindy's pregnancy amounted to one more weapon. Her mother wanted an abortion. Cindy wanted the baby. Her father, a guidance counselor and a secret drinker, wanted all of them to disappear, refusing even to accept the rape story. Cindy rode the Greyhound with a school nurse to Minneapolis, delivered a boy that she left in a foster home—and whose fate was to become wrapped up in the divorce tactics and thrusts of Mr. and Mrs. Riggs—and returned to begin her outlandish years, a period that continued through her marriage to the young widower, Potter.

Something woke Potter. He'd developed a tolerance to routine daytime noise, but this was different—a sharp crack, like wood breaking. It came from the hill, he was sure. Could someone be chopping down one of his trees? He stepped out on the porch, bare-chested. Ted Brekke's flatbed rolled by, spreading dust.

Potter circled the trailer, half asleep. Cyn had set out a bag of garbage—bones, soup cans, coffee grounds, wilted vegetables—and it lay strewn about, scattered by stray dogs.

As Potter climbed the hill the noise stopped. At the top he paused, admiring the treehouse. On the way down he spotted the birch. A small area about head-high appeared stained with sap, the papery bark worn away to expose a pulpy brown substance resembling the inside of a date-filled roll.

Potter spooned coffee crystals into a plastic cup as Cyn got home, a bag of groceries in each arm, curls fluttering. "You're up early," she said.

He spoke over the whistle of the kettle. "Not to scare you, but you haven't seen any strangers around?"

Cyn set the groceries on the counter, grimacing from the weight. "Your friend Bluto already asked. Him and Gene Granger came out the other night."

She opened the refrigerator and wedged in a half-gallon of milk next to an upside-down bottle of French dressing. She wadded an empty sack. "You sure have a taste for oranges lately."

"Oranges," Potter said. "I haven't eaten an orange all summer."

Cyn stuffed the sack in a drawer. "You forgot the garbage again. I told you the dogs'll get into it."

Potter checked the work orders left by the day shift against the quantities of flour stacked by the mixer conveyor. At three he turned the lights off in the main office and let Art out, leaving the key in the lock, the chain dangling.

Now came Potter's favorite time of night—the two hours between Art's cleaning and the arrival of the drivers. Working nights all these years, Potter liked to think that he existed in a negative and opposite dimension, one peculiar to his own idiosyncrasies. His working day started at midnight—the same as the ticks of the clock. He could whistle, sing, call himself a bastard. He could pray. His mind could spin as his hands worked, control panel to shelf, switch to conveyor, bin to hopper, directed only by their own memory.

A car turned the corner by the Sinclair station. Potter took the full flash of its twin beams in his eyes. He liked looking out the window. He found a power gained in watching people when they don't know they're being watched. He studied the vehicles passing: Bluto and Granger on the prowl for the troubled, tired waitresses heading home at last, citizens starting and ending their days. And teen-agers. Teen-agers own the night. The youthful part of the day for the youth of humanity. They have the beauty and the energy. They go without sleep, work long hours, play without restraint. They have the will and the strength to eat, drink, make love, and start the cycle again. Why not and good for them.

Potter came out of the rising room and set the timer for forty minutes. Just long enough for ginger cookies. He'd need cinnamon, cloves, unsalted butter from the cooler. He used a rubber spatula to cream the butter and sugar. He loved simple rituals, the repetitiveness, the sense of control. He was gratified that Olafson decided against total automation. Maybe when he took over he'd even do away with a few things, like frozen eggs and pre-mix.

He'd use his own yeast and only fresh ingredients. There could still be fun in baking, particularly in the preparation of small batches, specialties and custom orders. He loved getting his hands in the mix—he could probe the texture, sense its temperature and know that it was ready for the oven.

Potter was aware that it was not for his artistic creations that he'd some day run the bakery. The town stayed too small to make a go with walnut tarts and cherry chocolate mousse. This was a white bread place. Maybe one day he'd move to Minneapolis or San Francisco and start a specialty shop. He dreamed of running his own place, of organizing his day. Be good at something. That was what was important. But Potter also knew that the secret of success in dreams is the same as in pastries—knowing when to alter: when to cut the sugar, how the humidity feels, changing as you go to meet the changing demands.

As he reached for the molasses his arm hit the large mixing bowl. It struck a smaller bowl that spilled water on the open oven door producing a hiss and a small cloud of steam through which when it cleared, Potter came to a realization:

Someone's living in my treehouse.

The ginger cookies were flawless—an even brown, their surfaces dotted with sugar crystals that caught the overhead light like tiny prisms. Potter studied them. He once thought he'd invented this recipe, but then to his great disappointment he found it in a hand-written cookbook that once belonged to Cindy Riggs.

Someone in the treehouse?

Not long after Cindy moved away, Potter discovered he no longer smelled the rich bakery aroma he used to love, the sweet fragrances of spices and thick yeasty air. All disappeared along with a whole section of Potter's life. Six years yanked out. The things tied to his time with Cindy Riggs were heavy with memories: a blue Toyota that ran and ran, a big golden dog, Robert DeNiro's best movies. It wasn't fair that parallel events should have gone on unbothered. The Mets should be made to return the pennant. Two presidential elections ought to be canceled.

The phone jangled. Usually wrong numbers this time of night. He wiped his hands on his apron and grabbed the extension by the bulletin board.

It was Granger. "Just to let you know Cyn's all right, she had a scare is all."

"Where are you?"

"Your place. She thinks she saw somebody prowling around. Bluto's looking. You ought to put a light out there, Potter."

Something *was* askew in the treehouse. Potter sensed the rearrangement, an awareness of someone else's carbon dioxide, other beings folding themselves against the wall, pushing into a space that fit only him. He knew it even before he found the blanket and the orange peels.

He should call Bluto and Granger. Bluto would welcome it, settling the complaint of the neighbors, another chance to stomp ass. But the situation extended beyond a trespass to an implied compliment: someone was fond of his treehouse. Potter stretched out on the floor and waited, staring at lines of nails in the paneling, picking out mistakes only the builder would notice.

The same woody crack he'd heard before reached him. He sat up far enough to peek through the tiny gap between the frame and the window sill. Another item that needed fixing. A second crack sounded, then another.

The sumac parted. Potter watched, perched high in the air, aware of his own incongruity. This time they were right. It *was* a kid—a boy, pale and slight. He carried a kind of long string or cord looped around his right wrist.

The boy stared intently at the birch tree in front of him. Potter held his breath. The boy shook down the contraption from his wrist and carefully placed a rock in a pouch attached to the cord. He fastened his eyes on the tree for a concentrated second before his hand flew up and over his head. A whir filled the air, replaced by a solid *crack* as the rock hit the tree.

Potter watched as the boy picked up more rocks. There was something in the way he tucked his chin in against his shoulder. Potter studied him as he practiced from varying directions, marveling how the thin arm could produce such velocity. Rock after rock smacked the tree, each in the same spot. To see the boy use his sling was to appreciate excellence. Potter found himself fascinated. A panel truck rattled by on the road below. The boy slipped into the woods. Potter made his way back down the hill.

When Cyn left for work the next day Potter changed into his sneakers and walked a quarter-mile past Proutys where the dog raised his head and barked, turned north at the corner, walked another quarter-mile, hiked east, then cut in along the swampy-smelling willow bog. The warm air beaded perspiration on the back of his bare neck. He reached the back of the hill, his steps becoming livelier with the excitement of stealth.

The peak of the treehouse roof came into view. He sat down in the thick grass to wait, brushing bugs from his bare arms while trying to decide what he might say. Shortly a foot appeared on the top rung, then another. The boy reached the ground and stretched.

He was a raggedy kid with a narrow face that appeared to be trying to trigger a recognition in Potter. His jeans were furrowed with wrinkles at the hip and around the knees. The Keds showed grass and mud-stains, but his T-shirt looked clean.

Potter stood and walked into the clearing. The boy gave a start, but didn't move. The sling dangled from his arm.

"Hi," Potter said.

The boy nodded.

"My name's Carl, but I go by my last name. Potter."

"Right," the boy said, blinking.

"I'm the guy that lives in the trailer."

"Yeah, I saw you before." Rich, blond hair descended over the boy's ears. He toyed with the sling, coiling it into a ball.

Up close the shadowy familiarity disappeared. "Did you want to tell me your name?"

"Anthony," the boy said.

"Anthony. Oh, Tony then?"

"Nope—just Anthony."

"Well, tell me Anthony, is it that you're running away or what?"

The boy didn't answer.

Potter wanted to open up a circle of conversation, a space to get acquainted, seek the thing in the way people grope around with words and ideas that would make Anthony feel comfortable. He put a hand on the ladder, wiggling it. "How long you been staying out here, in my treehouse?"

Anthony watched Potter, as if waiting to see whether he intended to climb the ladder. "I thought you wouldn't care," he said. He picked up a rock, fitted it in the sling and let fly at the bruised birch.

"Nice shot," Potter said. "But maybe you should practice on a dead tree."

"Oh, I didn't think."

"You look sort of familiar. You live in Lakota?"

"Nope, I'm passing through. I was thinking about leaving."

"And where you from?"

"Around Minnesota. Back down there."

"Is that so? Well, can I help you out with anything?"

"Nope."

The next morning when Potter climbed the hill with two cans of pop and a loaf of Russian rye sliced and stuffed with cheese and ham, he found the door latched and the blanket gone. A towel was wrapped around the wounded tree and tied tightly with a square knot.

Potter folded the newspaper open on the counter. Olafson's daughter Kaye was getting married. Potter remembered Kaye as a lisping six-year old, begging him for chocolate chips. Now a photo showed her full grown, standing behind her fiance with her hands resting on his shoulders.

Bluto pushed through the side door, wearing a plastic rain protector over his cop's hat. "They say he's a baker, Potter."

Potter didn't look up. "Too bad we got no openings."

"Seriously. I heard that." Bluto skirted past Potter, shedding a trail of raindrops. "Let me have a couple of them jelly longjohns."

Potter turned the page. "You eat too much."

Bluto worked his way around the counter. "You shouldn't insult this part of the law, Potter. Say you're the victim of a treehouse burglary. Off the top of my head I'd say you could be s.o.l."

"Am I worried?"

"You ought to be. Your girlfriend's scared silly."

Potter looked up. "Of what? There's nothing out there."

"That ain't what she told Geno."

"Well she hasn't told me."

A stubble of whisker stood out white against Bluto's red chin. "Now you got me wondering, Potter. I mean if it's dope or something. You know, we're old friends. She calls us every night. What's going on?"

"For a moment the custom of being agreeable worked on Potter. But this was stupid old Bluto—who'd stolen his radio in sixth grade. All he could recollect at the moment was that Bluto had a birthmark shaped like Florida on his left buttock. He wished he were in his treehouse. "You got me. I work nights, remember?"

On their last Memorial Day together Potter and Cindy Riggs had visited the cemetery. Cynthia's grave was in the new section where the markers were flush with the ground. They stood quietly, staring at the reddish gravestone with its plain, block lettering:

A FEW MORE TOILS, A FEW MORE TEARS
AND WE SHALL WEEP NO MORE

"It's got my name," Cindy said. "I should have stayed Riggs. I could die with this name too. Then what would you do?"

"Find another Cynthia."

"You jerk," she said, tugging on his hand.

At home Potter ran tap water over an aluminum strainer filled with Bing cherries. He carried it to Cindy along with a paper towel. "Maybe we'll take a trip this summer, go out west," he said, flicking drops of water at her face.

"I won't hold my breath," she said, spitting a stone at his shoe.

The papers had come certified mail from an address listing five names on Simi Boulevard, Los Angeles, California. The cover letter said that if Potter would sign in the designated places, Cynthia Potter, who was petitioning to become Cynthia Riggs again, promised to relinquish any claim on their jointly held property. Potter took the papers and his checkbook in to Dick Charleton who assured him that yes, that was the case.

Potter uncapped his ballpoint. "What happens if I don't sign?"

Dick nibbled a thumbnail and checked it through his glasses. "We're talking real estate that she'll give up free and clear. That's nice acreage you have out there."

Of the boys in Potter's class only Dick returned to Lakota after going

away to college. It felt strange asking him for advice—and stranger yet
paying for it. "Say she comes back, then what?"

"As long as the marriage contract's in effect everything's half hers. Plus
you're not free to remarry."

Potter looked at the papers again. All that raised lettering and black
print failed to make the situation any prettier. "What about her name?"

"Means nothing. She can use any name she wants. Knowing Cindy I
imagine she'll use Riggs no matter what you want."

Potter folded the papers back into the brown envelope. "Thanks Dick.
I'll have to think about it. What do I owe you?"

Dick pushed himself up by the arms of his chair. "A dozen of your
strawberry tarts—so far. The next I'm giving free."

"The next—what's that?"

"Potter, she's not coming back."

Cindy Riggs sent hand-painted post cards signed *love always* for two years.
By the time they stopped Cyn had moved in.

Cyn once worked at the bakery, though when she and Potter started
sleeping together she'd gotten on as a checker at Red Owl. Potter's reverse
manner of living hadn't bothered her. She seemed amused that he rushed
off to work after they made love. The first item she kept at the trailer
was a mascara kit. Others followed, spare curling iron, special conditioner,
blow dryer, until they realized she'd moved in. "May as well save the rent,"
she said. "I'll probably need it some day."

Potter spoke into the bathroom door. "I'm going up to work on the
treehouse."

"I can't hear you. What?"

"The *tree*house," he said. "I need to seal it up good before it gets cold."

Cyn opened the door. She wore the pink bathrobe abandoned by Cindy
Riggs. Potter guessed she'd find Dentyne wrappers, plastic book marks,
and who knows—a lock of hair from the Dalai Lama—left in the pockets.

Cyn toweled her hair, speaking into her lap. "How did my chest-of-drawers
get that scratch?"

Potter couldn't deflect his irritation. "*Your* chest-of-drawers? Do I ever
say *my* fridge, *my* Contac paper, *my* electricity?"

"What's wrong with you?" she said, brushing past him to the bedroom, closing the door behind her.

The treehouse offered a warm look. Before Potter reached the ladder he knew Anthony was back. He sat and waited. When Cyn's car pulled away the boy stepped into the clearing.

"Passing through again?" asked Potter.

"I got scared those cops would come up."

Potter stood, slapping dust from his pants. "You hungry?"

Anthony shrugged, unwinding his sling.

"Let's go down to the trailer—it's okay."

Potter found a frozen pizza under Cyn's diet dinners. He added mozzarella, tomato sauce, oregano and thin pieces of pepperoni sliced from a ring. "Some things need a special improving touch," he said, opening the oven. "So you're going home?"

Anthony sat at the kitchen table, watching the oven. "There is no home," he said.

To Potter, Anthony appeared more substantial indoors. A city boy. Too much of nature overwhelmed him. "It's getting cold. You probably got state patrols looking for you. I wouldn't be surprised to see your picture on our bread wrappers."

"Are you looking to turn me in?"

So he *is* a runaway, Potter thought. They could have him back in Minnesota tomorrow. "That depends." Potter imagined Bluto puffing up the hill. "Are you worth anything?"

Anthony smiled. "Cripes man. What do you think?"

"No charges, crimes?"

"No nothing."

"Do you pick your nose?"

"Just in counties where it's legal."

Potter pulled the pizza from the oven, slid it onto the cutting board and carved out wide wedges with the cleaver. He set the whole thing in front of Anthony. "Go ahead, I'll open some Cokes."

Anthony took a slice, blew on it and started chewing as Potter watched. He continued eating without speaking. When he finished Potter brought a bowl of rice pudding from the refrigerator.

"Listen," Potter said. "I got to get some rest."

Anthony ran his finger around the bowl. "I don't sleep so good myself. Always waking up." He licked his finger. "But nothing against your treehouse. Best one I ever saw."

"Really? Everyone wonders what it's for since I got no kids."

"No, I like that. In Minnesota there's this guy who built his own helicopter—and he doesn't know how to fly. Do things for the heck of it. Don't you think?" Anthony closed the door, then knocked and opened it. "One thing," he said. "If you expect us travelers to get really comfortable up there a bathroom wouldn't hurt."

Potter had mentioned to Cindy Riggs that he hated passing the corner by the John Deere agency where the first Cynthia had the accident.

"You were born here," she said. "I suppose you can't visit the house where your dad had the heart attack. And somebody's bound to have run over your bike. How do you think I feel about St. Paul? Just keep putting new things in place of the old."

Potter kissed her on the nose, then on the lips. "But some of the old just can't be replaced," he said.

When Cindy did go Potter began a vigorous study of ways to become independent. He envisioned a windmill for electricity, a wood stove for heat, and an underground storage compartment for vegetables. He walked the property, trying to figure out where to build a greenhouse. Back-to-the-land would save him.

"How about your parents—you get along?"

A rock flew. "What do you think?"

Potter gazed toward the hill, not speaking. Quaking aspen blazed the crest with orange and yellow.

"I should say I get along with my mother—at least I did during the hour and a half we spent together."

"Your dad?"

"Never met the guy." Anthony unraveled his sling, stretched it, checking the rawhide for nicks. "So now I'm going to see my mother again."

"And she knows you're coming?"

"Not really."

"How about the people in Minnesota?"

"How about 'em."

"So you ran away from your—what, grandma? And you're on your way to check out your mother."

"I got no grandma either. Least ways one that I ever heard much good about."

"Then let's call your mother. Tell her you're all right."

Anthony shook his head. "Not yet."

"It's okay," Potter said. "I'll tell you what. Two more days I got the weekend off and Cyn works. That gives you time to think about what you could say, and we'll call her then. For now be a little more careful. You're scaring Cyn."

"Cyn. You mean like Cindy?"

Potter nodded. "I could tell you stories."

"She's pretty."

"She is. Wish I could figure why she gets mad when I tell her that."

"Maybe it's how you say it."

"Someone else told me that once."

Anthony wiped his forehead with the back of his wrist. "You know how we been the last couple days? That's the most I ever talked to anyone old as you."

Potter liked the quickening of late summer. Already the path lay strewn with yellowing fan-shaped ginkgo leaves. "I brought rolls for later," he said.

The boy sorted through an assortment of rocks, flipping the rejects to the side. Potter watched the slender hands at work, making a mental note to pick up a fingernail clipper. "So what do you think—we call your mother today?"

Anthony had set up four Hamm's cans on the stump, side by side. He stepped back, sighted, and twirled his sling. Each can fell with a single shot. It was a particular kind of genius. "Nope," he said.

"But they're bound to report you missing. This is a small town. The cops here can be awful touchy."

Anthony lowered himself to the ground, sitting in the ginkgo leaves, his knees jutting. "Remember I said she don't know I'm coming. I wanted to talk to you about that."

Potter knew it was only a matter of time before he'd be hit up for a loan—to be repaid, presumably, by the mother. "And?"

"I want to know if you'll come with me."

Potter's gaze focused on Anthony's bony white knee, visible through a rent in the jeans. "Come with you?"

Anthony nodded. "Yeah. You see, you already know my mother."

Potter gave the boy a searching look, trying to make sense. A jolt hit his powers of realization. He calculated years. *Could this be right?* "Are you telling me . . ."

"You married her."

"But you're almost grown up . . ."

"I'm fourteen. She was sixteen."

Potter studied the boy as if for the first time. Knobby elbows, ungraceful posture and bearing. That must come from his father, but there sure was a lot of Cindy Riggs in the face. Here existed a living connection between the symbols of words and the enormity of ideas.

"You'd be my stepson."

Anthony smiled, his thin face glowing. "Yup. If the two of you hadn't blown it."

Potter watched Anthony eating Cheerios. Half a box in a mixing bowl. Down the hatch with a soup spoon, a heap at a time.

"How come you didn't tell me this right away?"

Anthony shook his head. There was no denying the eyes. "Well, for one reason, the first thing I noticed was all the cops around here."

"It just looks that way when you're on the move."

"That's good. I was afraid maybe they were your friends."

Potter offered more Cheerios. "I don't recall your mom calling you Anthony."

The boy spoke through a full mouth. "Middle name."

"Oh yes. Thomas, right?"

It's good you hang around me, Potter. You're getting smarter."

Potter slid a chair out, turned it backward and straddled it. "You know, used to be I couldn't mention you but that she'd start to cry."

Anthony refilled the bowl. "You're making that up to make me feel good, right?"

Potter shook his head. "Wrong."

"She wrote lots of letters after you and her split. I know quite a bit about you."

"Like what?"

"Oh, you're a top baker. You had a wife that got killed and her name was Cindy too. Stuff like that. That you're a good guy and all. She said people take advantage of you with money."

"She said that? It's not so."

"Don't blame me. She never mentioned much bad. In case you were wondering."

"I was, sort of."

"She said when you guys were together you never wanted to take vacations. And like that. You'd never even seen the ocean."

"It's true. I still haven't."

"Yeah? Don't you think it's time? Not that you're old. At least very. Even though you're gettin' bald."

"Good of you to notice," said Potter, watching Anthony eat, remembering how as a teen-ager he'd devour three sweet rolls between the time clock and the bakery front door.

"So I guess her wanting to get around more was something you got in fights about?"

"I just realized," said Potter. "We hardly ever fought."

"Then you shouldn't have split. Right?

Potter shrugged. "So she never brought you to live with her after all."

"I thought you knew that."

"Who's been raising you then?"

"Foster families, same as before."

"Your mother, did she ever mention much else about us breaking up?"

"I think it was mostly cause she didn't want to live here anymore."

Potter took a deep breath. "No, Anthony. It was mostly over you."

"Me?"

"Isn't that something?" Potter said. "I didn't want you here, and because of it she's gone." He stood. His chair scraped the floor. "And here you are."

"And here I am."

Potter scooped vanilla ice cream into a soup bowl. "So you're on your way to see her. She's still in L.A. then."

"No. She moved."

Potter smiled, thinking of frantic Cindy, loading her suitcases with half a ton of books she wouldn't read. "Where'd she move to?"

Anthony worked his Adam's apple up and down, swallowing ice cream. "Nepal."

The window glass facing the road blurred in Potter's peripheral vision. *Nepal? Now what,* he thought. "Tell me, Anthony. How much money you got, rounded off."

"Oh—I'm not sure. Few hundred maybe."

"Not that round."

"Okay. A little less."

"Nepal. Nepal. Jesus. The country of Nepal?"

"No, the rock band. What do you think?"

"I shouldn't be surprised, but what's she doing there?"

"She helps them grow food and things. You ever heard about this bunch called Help the Children . . . something or other?"

"*Save* the Children. Well, how do you like that?"

"I don't like it too good, Potter. Considering."

"Anthony, we better figure out a whole bunch of stuff. We're looking at passports, visas, big money. We got to re-talk Minnesota."

"I don't want foster homes," said Anthony. "Please. You don't know."

When Art left Potter took the phone book to the office, studying the listings. Mexico. Monaco. Netherlands. Where to start?

Lately Bluto had taken to stopping in during the night, mostly without Granger who was busy at the station with reports. Potter wished it were the other way around, with Granger coming in. He needed advice, wished he had someone to talk to. So many years of night-shift solitude brought a price.

Usually Potter let Bluto go about finding his own pastry and coffee. Tonight with the mixer already churning he poured coffee for himself also and sat down. "Say, you ever get tired of Lakota?" he asked.

Bluto stopped chewing. "Why you asking? Things not going so good with Olafson?"

"All of us past thirty now. I just never guessed we'd still be living here."

Bluto jabbed himself in the chest with his thumb. "Well I wouldn't live nowhere else and be a cop. The way it's getting in your cities a police officer can't even do his job but he's got to worry about these rights and those rights. Being a cop's easy in Lakota. Departments out in California never even answer our telexes, that's how much they got to do."

"Really? I wonder what it's like for pastry cooks."

"Forget it, Potter. They'll bury us here. Which reminds me, when we get that kid I'll take him for a ride, you won't see him around Lakota no more."

"How many times I got to tell you guys you're wasting the taxpayers' money? There's nothing up there but a couple stray dogs."

Bluto burped softly. "You sound like the council. They don't like us going out there so we do it on our own. We'll see one of these nights if you're right. Geno wants to try a stake-out."

Anthony unraveled his sling as they broke through the brush onto the road. "You know what I spend a lot of time thinking about? If that had never happened to my mom I wouldn't even be on this planet." He fired a rock at the Speed Limit sign. It struck with a clang, rattling the coat of summer dust and bird droppings.

"What did I just say about noise," said Potter. "Come on, let's get back in the trees."

To Potter the world couldn't make sense. Good can come out of bad. Somebody's completely selfish instincts produced Anthony. "But I thought light-skinned males were in demand," he said.

"Yeah if they're two years old. You know my mother, she would never sign the papers. The way they explained it was she always meant to send for me when she got things together."

"So what *are* we going to do with you? Whatever it is, it's got to be soon now."

Anthony pushed through a cluster of leaves on the path. "Why can't you come with me?"

"For about a hundred reasons. First, I've got someone here. Second, I can't leave a job I've been doing all these years. People my age—we just can't make ourselves act on whims. And third. Well, do you even know where Nepal is at?"

Anthony paused, jamming his hands in his pockets. "I guess I better tell you something. She's not there anymore."

"What do you mean?"

"Please Potter, if I said St. Paul or L.A. you'd right away make the calls and get rid of me. This way I got more time. To spend here."

Potter drew a deep breath. "Well where is she then?"

"L.A."

Potter sensed his anger rising. "I don't think so. The day after you told me I got hold of the West Coast Save the Children headquarters. There's no Cindy Riggs on their register."

"Riggs," said Anthony, as if the name tasted of vinegar. "That's my grandparents. I hate that name."

Potter grew light-headed. "Oh God, am I stupid. She's still *Potter*."

"Of course. Why wouldn't she be?"

Les Prouty's beat-up Scout rumbled past on the road below. "Let's find a place to sit down."

"Then you're thinking about it?"

Potter rubbed the back of his neck. "The problem with you is you don't listen."

Anthony's voice sounded lower. "*You* don't listen. What's wrong with not having plans? You gonna live in a treehouse the rest of your life? No wonder Mom split."

That stung, but Potter let it go. He admired the determination. "Just now you could use a little planning. And what about Cyn?"

"Mom?"

"Forget your mother for a minute. The one I've been living with for two years. It's getting to feel the same as married."

"Does she think it's the same?"

"What do you mean?"

"A cop visits at night, when you're at work."

"Because you couldn't keep out of sight."

"Twice this week, Potter. And for sure they never saw me."

Potter listened, rolling the facts in his mind. He had a sudden longing for the world he knew best, the two o'clock in the morning world—the one where he was awake, alive, and alone, loving the comfort of his ritual, ready to work his problems to death while others gave in to theirs. He sighed. "You want to tell me more about it?"

"I can even tell you what they talk about."

Potter broke a dead branch over his knee. "I don't think I want to know."

"Back down, Potter. I just did it once. She was complaining about the water and how it's no good for her hair."

Potter nodded. "Well hell. She says the same stuff to him she does to me. You're sure it's a cop."

Anthony pulled on his lip, thinking. "One lets the other out, then comes back and gets him."

"How long's he stay?"

"I don't know. Half hour."

Potter studied Anthony's face, seeing the blue eyes of Cindy Riggs. "This is for sure now."

"Honest."

"What's he look like?"

"The one in the car's fat."

"Anthony, I appreciate you telling me this, but you know it can't change anything. Like I said, they know about you. You need to go. Soon."

Anthony jammed his hands in his pockets. "Too bad I got only one parent."

"Yeah, well. Ever think about your father?"

"All the time for a while. Once on TV they had Charles Manson's son and I heard him say his dad was an evil force. How does *he* know? Oh, I'll never talk to my dad or nothing. But I used to wonder if once or twice maybe he's driving along listening to that old music like the Beatles and he sees these kids getting out of school. And he wonders if one of them is his son or daughter. And just in case he gives this little wave, you know, of good luck. I bet my father's not as bad a guy as Charles Manson, you think?"

Potter swallowed, turning away. "I'm sure," he said.

"And Potter?"

"Yeah."

"I never meant that about Mom. She really loves you."

"Where's your partner?"

"Damn! I didn't see you in the dark there." Bluto wiped his hands on his trousers. "Book work," he said. "They made it so we got to type our own reports. City's getting tight."

Potter leaned against the refrigerator case, feeling the cool against his shoulder, watching Bluto rearrange himself.

Bluto folded his hands around his coffee mug, like a man at a campfire. "Don't you got work? Usually you're busy this time of night."

"I have a favor to ask."

Bluto shifted his weight on the bench. "Favor?"

"Let me know when you pull this stake-out. I want to be there."

Bluto tore his jelly roll in half and licked his fingers. "No can do, Potter. That's police business. Guy like you might get hurt. I seen how you are around guns."

"I'll chance it."

"Like I said, we're not even . . ."

"All I want to know is when."

Bluto chewed and swallowed quickly, his mouth working. "No, we'd be in deep shit."

Potter stood away from the case. "Wouldn't be tonight, would it?"

"Stay out of it."

A spout in the cleaning room vented steam with a sudden hiss. "You tub of lard, it is tonight."

"Goddamn," Bluto choked. "What's got into you?"

Couldn't Art for once in his life *not* sweep under the farthest corners of the racks and maybe leave five minutes early? Evidently not. Potter sighed.

Cyn answered on the first ring. "Oh, it's you! I thought it'd be Bluto," she said. "Gene snuck up the back way and thinks he saw somebody. Bluto went in to get the big flashlights. I *told* you somebody was up there."

From the time Cynthia had the accident, Potter knew that it took eight minutes to shut down all the valves. He hit the main power switch, dropped the bar on the delivery door, and grabbed his jacket with the two paychecks in the pocket. As he backed out of his parking space Bluto rounded the corner by the bank.

Potter followed in the Chevy, arriving to see Bluto heft himself from the squad car, gun in one hand, flashlight in the other. When he saw Potter pulling up behind he waited, tapping his flashlight on the side of his leg. "Either stay here or go inside," he said.

The key alarm whined as Potter opened his door. He nudged the door closed with his foot. "It's all right," he said.

Granger stepped from the trailer porch, pointing to the trail. Potter called to him. "I know who it is." He sensed Cyn peeking through the Thermopane window, the door bolted.

"Bluto, let's do this one right," said Granger.

But Bluto had already moved uphill, climbing quickly for a big man. "Hurry up, for Christ's sake," he yelled over his shoulder. Twigs cracked beneath his heavy shoes. The beam of the flashlight darted about the brush, casting graceful angles of interwoven black. He halted at the first clearing, puffing, hands on his knees.

Potter followed, stumbling and picking his way with no flashlight, keeping Bluto in sight. He tried again. "I'll talk to him, all right?"

"Bullshit too. He'll just get away again." Bluto crouched as he moved out of the clearing. "Wait there, I know right where he's at."

Potter tripped over a root and tripped again. Why was Granger so slow? *Cyn,* he realized. "You don't need the gun, Bluto. It's a kid."

Bluto paused, framed between two slender oaks, scanning the higher ground. His twisted face became pallid, as if his skin absorbed everything— the night air, the silence of the woods, the yellow moonlight. "Step out where I can see you," he shouted between breaths.

Potter worked his way through heavy brush with his elbow protecting his face, losing his bearings for a moment. Three long strides and Bluto came in sight again, his cap on the back of his head, his gun directed upward.

"This'll shake him out," said Bluto. A fierce blue light, an explosion. *Wham!* A shower of dry leaves crackled to the ground.

Potter grabbed the rough bark of a boxelder with his palm, pulling himself closer. "Bluto, please. Listen."

Bluto turned to face Potter. "I'm gonna tell you . . ." A whirring noise interrupted—followed by a *thunk!* like a jar of honey striking a concrete floor. Bluto dropped the flashlight, grunted, and sagged to his side on the lumpy ground.

Something moved in the trees. "Anthony! Don't come out," yelled Potter, trying to spot Bluto's gun.

Lifting one hand, Bluto dabbed his forehead with a finger, then sprawled flat on his belly, his gun useless at his side.

Granger ran up, breathless, his head low and his hand on his holster. "What the hell was that?"

"A rock. Hurry up."

Granger knelt over Bluto, and rolled him onto his back. "Here, get his feet elevated. You know how to use the radio?"

Potter shook his head. He held the flashlight as Granger pressed a rag to Bluto's forehead.

Granger sat back on his haunches. "We'll have to tell Cyn to phone. They'll need the portable. Who *is* that anyway?"

Potter hesitated, wondering how to answer. "My boy," he said.

"Who?"

Potter glanced at Bluto's darkening wound. "How is he?"

"Well, head cuts bleed a lot. His pupils look normal."

Anthony stepped from behind a tree to the left, holding his sling. "He was gonna shoot you," he said, his voice a whimper. He edged closer. Potter wrapped his free arm around him.

Granger glanced at Anthony. "Better get him down to the car."

Potter felt the boy stiffen. "Gene, I never asked you for a thing."

Granger wiped his hands in the leaves. "Are you now?"

Potter pulled Anthony closer. "I am."

Granger took off his cap. "You don't get anything, do you? I didn't say which car."

Potter swallowed. "If I could get some things out of the trailer."

Granger slid his sleeve up and read his watch. "Give her a flashlight and tell her I need help. Make it quick. I'll get you an hour, two at the most." He made a pillow of Bluto's cap, resting it under his neck. "I guess we owe it to you."

Buckled into the Chevy's soft seat, the warm air from the heater blowing over him, Anthony at last quit trembling.

Potter eased up on the accelerator. "Think we can find her?" he asked, after a long thoughtful silence.

Anthony opened his eyes, stretched, and fell back asleep without answering.

They drove on, the rising sun visible in the rearview mirror. Potter gazed at the scrub grass on the passing hillside, reflecting on the other more familiar hill they'd left behind, and how the outline of the treehouse roof emerged barely visible through the leafless limbs of the trees as they pulled away. He wished he'd mounted a weather vane on that sturdy roof. He could see it now, glinting in the light as it turned with the wind, pointing to all the infinite directions in the world.

Painting Over Christ

YOU DO *things.*

Many's the time I asked Aggie why she would climb in a hammock with a guy like Hooknose Howard Habicek but she won't say. Some questions got no answer. You looked at Hooknose you saw five feet of slime and eight inches of hair. We hated him. Hooknose used to pelt fire trucks with tomatoes he filched from Ziggy's—so Ziggy hated him too, not to mention the firemen.

But the fact of the matter is Aggie and Hooknose did do it. Before we got married. In Aggies's backyard over on Kimball. It's true. I made her tell me.

Maybe you have events in your life you want to forget. Like when I says to Aggie once back before I give her the ring, "Didja hear Mick Jagger died?"

Aggie started loadin' her Coke with reds before I got around to saying, *Yeah,* it was a bag of blowhard. No harm done.

You're supposed to act guilty for such a sin you could wipe away with three *Our Fathers?* At least my old man knew better.

He was a barber, my old man. That's how he got his livelihood, giving two-dollar crew cuts—the Lucky Tiger tonic he threw in for free. Twenty-two years he rode the Ravenswood El to his shop on Armitage. Every Saturday night he ate piroshki and drank German beer from black glass bottles.

My old man got around. He shook the hand of Daley. He used to go to the stadium when they had Bobby Hull, and he knew a guy was at the Blackhawk the night they named "Big Noise from Winnetka" after the mouthy little shits from the suburbs. Good-hearted too. Cops and priests got ten percent, never mind the precinct. Keep the lines open, he said. The thing was, fashion's hair turned him mean. Short, long—who can keep up?

And he was smart. He could name you places you never heard of. He read everything came in the shop. All the latest *National Geographics* he'd take and put in the ammo case he used for a foot rest by his chair when it got slow. I figure that's where he first heard about Greenland, a place you could leave your past behind.

One day he took me aside. Talking through the smoke of his Chesterfield he tells me the shop's down the tubes, but he's got this plan. He's gonna spread gas around the storage closet and leave a lit cigarette in a match book. "They won't find *nothin'* wasn't supposed to be there," he said.

How he knew how to do that is anybody's guess. Such facts don't come out of *Field and Stream*.

For me the problem got to be Aggie's carping. She claimed she married me for better than I showed her as a house painter. Every paycheck she was wantin' another silk top from Carson's or stiletto heels like her friend Louise wore.

I was a good painter too. Jobs asked for me by name, but the union was something else. They had this apprentice from Kenosha got me written up. For smoking. Yeah, that's what they come to in the union now. The precinct captain had to get me back in. But first he made me promise no more over smoking will I rip buttons off the shirt of a prick from Kenosha.

Then I got the chance to go to Greenland. My old man heard about a guy comes back with heavy sugar, cash of the kind you don't show at Mama Luna's. The old man tells him stop by our place and let his son know what to write on the papers. And who shows up? Hooknose Howard Habicek. Grown up now. Still five feet of slime but an extra three inches of hair and a beer belly too. So good old Aggie popped him a pilsner anyhow, and first thing you know we got to be friends. Us and Hooknose.

The U.S. Air Force keeps planes and stuff at Greenland. Don't ask me why. Must be the generals figure the enemy won't look in such a place.

Anyway, the airmen up there look good in their blue ties and tan shirts, but when the parade is over they puke in the hallways and jam the toilets with socks. They're not the type that keep our country free, those airmen.

You find a lot of violet and black on the walls of the barracks at Greenland. Magic markers in those colors are issued same as tooth paste. The airmen take them and write bible stuff. *Hanc Igitur. Giving Thanks He Blessed It. Sursum Corda.* Words like that but nice things too. Poems that rhyme, and pictures. Lots of those airmen could have been something if not for the U.S. Air Force.

There was this building, the Crucifixion Barracks they called it, and my old man would of loved it. Those fliers had a thing for Jesus—being up in the air so much maybe had something to do with it. Every wall had one kind or other picture of Jesus—marching to the mountain, stuck on the cross. This or that, eating supper. They had him in every size, wallet to actual, all done with magic markers. In my favorite you could see his sacred heart in the center with lines beaming out like radio waves from that place on Belmont. It was to show love of the earth, and only the violet eyes bothered you. I felt like I was blotting out my own faith when I ran the roller over Jesus—halo, eyes, heart, and all.

I like to paint. There's a good feeling at the end of a job if you did it right. I'll tell you how you know if painting's the work of a pro like me. Look at the spots on a painter's glasses. They should be tiny, no bigger than the egg of a fly. I hate to see big drops. I know that here was a so-called painter who was careless in his work. It's like a saliva bubble on the corner of someone's lip. The person might be saying the pledge to the flag, but all you wish is he'd wipe his goddamn mouth. So it is with me and paint spots larger than the egg of a fly.

My old man lost his faith when they didn't want crew cuts no more. He drank too much and it gave him bad judgment. Alcohol, the enemy of good sense. In Greenland I was waiting for news the shop burnt up, but the old man never got the chance. One night he reached to brush a spider off the collar of a stockbroker at the Fullerton El stop. Someone pushed, the next one shoved. My old man tripped and along came the Evanston Express.

Good old Aggie. She told me he hit the third rail when he tumbled and never felt a thing. Later on I talked to someone was there. He says my old man grabbed the stockbroker's sleeve and about pulled him down with him, and then in the middle of nothing but air he got him back. Called the bastard a *motherfucker*. Such was his last words.

You need good reasons to go to Greenland. Turns out Hooknose had a habit of marrying waitresses from the Old Town clubs. He kissed the neck of his wives in public, but at home he grabbed their wrists and shouted in their face. They stayed with him twelve weeks tops, long enough so's the dental kicked in, then they got their teeth fixed and maybe a trip to Orlando. It was savage the way those wives went through Hooknose. I can name you three women right now walking around Old Town with terrific teeth, courtesy of Hooknose Howard.

Greenland treated me good. We got nylon brushes and laborers to tape and sand. I met painters from all over the globe—New Mexico, Canada, Des Moines Iowa. We played bumper pool and checked out Chuck Norris movies from the commissary. If you had the time they even offered books. We ate buttered muffins in the morning and chicken at night. Chicken every dinnertime, compliments of the U.S. Air Force.

I should never of left, but all the chicken in Greenland won't make up for when your old man falls off the El platform. And you get lonesome. Talking to Aggie was like calling from the moon—all static and squeaky. I kept telling her I loved her, figuring she could make those words out easy. Courtesy is a thing that exists on the phone, but all she ever said back was about going to bingo with Louise and could I maybe send more money.

Anyone thinks Greenland is green probably figures the dead don't vote in the forty-third ward. After a while you're sick of pool and the chicken's tasting like drywall. Guys are startin' to sniff their magic markers just to see what happens. Anything to get them through the long Greenland night. The rest are messing with their toes, rubbing them with turpentine. Seems like all the painters in Greenland got toe misfortunes. Corns and warts. Stuff you never heard of. No more can I pass the Dr. Sholl's without thinking of Greenland painters chewing on drumsticks and bitching about their toes.

So when I heard from the precinct captain he'd get me back on a job as a favor to my old man's memory, I counted my money and got myself signed out of Greenland.

The first clue was Aggie meeting the plane in a Kansas City Royals T-shirt. I hate the goddamn Kansas City Royals and she knew it. They got a waterfall behind the center field fence. You expect Judy Garland to sing for batting practice. I went there once with my best friend Stan who moved to Joliet. We watched Fisk go oh-for-five, and on the way back they picked me up for drunk. Aggie meant something with that T-shirt.

Aggie's other slip-up was talking too much about Hooknose Howard. Howie did this. Howie did that. Howie had to go to Warshawsky's to get seat covers for his new pickup. Howie got burned cause he forgot to use his sunscreen. Howie dumped yogurt on Louise's red jumper.

Other things told me the score. Bicycle experts like me know you gotta rotate the tires on a standing bike. First Aggie claimed she always done it. But I knew. Could be Hooknose told her rims don't need it. Like my old man always said, a turd will show its true color. But I know if you lie about small things you will lie about the big. Aggie used her own judgment. That's just as bad. Loved ones in marriage contracts should take the advice of the opposite who knows, rims being one of my fields.

I quit speaking to Hooknose, but thoughts about him kept coming to me. I'd imagine the good-for-nothing assface leaning against his truck, stripped to the waist and tryin' to hold in his slob belly. Then along would come Aggie, wearing her Royals T-shirt. Married to me she was, but reaching for Howie. Howie with his seat covers from Warshawsky's and his tender skin.

Aggie claimed she loved me, but she never said it just right. It was more the way you'd say that once you ate eggplant. Other things happened. I found perfume in her purse and flowery panties in her drawer. And when Louise came over they talked about things I don't know, like coriander and diamels.

We used to bike to Oak Street Beach, me and Aggie, even in the winter. Now Aggie rode with other people, and when she came home her hair smelled like cigarettes and her mouth smelled like gin.

"But why you so suspicious?" she said.

I told her. "Fidelity needs protection same as any other property."
She said fidelity was not my biggest worry.

Everyone makes mistakes. I admit to mine, others should do the same.
My worst mistake was *not* in sneaking around Hooknose's place like
Magnum P.I. trying to figure if he knew someone from Kansas City. It
wasn't even when the pallet of five-gallon cans issued to my crew got swiped.
It was in what happened when I got blamed for it.

I have a high IQ. What it is I ain't saying. Numbers are not important—
you have to be quick, too. So when the shop steward called me a moron
he was wrong. And to prove it I popped the sonofabitch with a claw bar.

He hit the deck quiet, with blood running down his cheek. Couple
a carpenters grabbed my arms and someone called security. But first thing
I know the steward's sittin' up with his hand on his goddamn ear.

"I'm glad you done that," he said. "And I guess you must a liked Greenland
cause that's the only place you're gonna get a job long as I'm steward."

So now I was a man with time on his hands, and I started pedaling by
Hooknose's place every time Aggie went out. Pretty soon I figured how
to get into the garage and I noticed Hooknose never bothered to latch
the door going into the house.

The night the Sox played KC for first place I stopped in at Kelly's Tavern
to watch it on their dish. I got a start when I pushed open the door. Two
men in straw hats stared at me. When I saw they were cardboard cutouts
for a booze display, I knew the joke was on me, and when the Sox went
nine runs down in the fifth I bought a couple a cartons of the peach stuff
they were selling and got the hell out before something worse happened.

I drank four of my peaches sitting on the swing at Humboldt Park,
and when that got uncomfortable I found a place on the grass under the
cannon. A couple strolled by. The woman said someone would get hurt
if they didn't fix the fence. The man said there were sure lots of whores
in Milwaukee. I drank the last of my peaches. When I got home Aggie
was gone, so I figured it was time to bike by Hooknose's again.

I was rickety from my peach drinks, but I pushed those pedals hard.
Every yard I passed had a chubby guy in his undershirt hosing grass and
every open window pumped the same salsa music into the night. I wheeled

up Damen and cut behind Wally's Vienna stand and caught the good smell
of onions frying on a hot grill. I waved at a bunch of black kids hangin'
like vines from a graveyard fence and I gave the finger to a pizza driver
who honked. Above me I could see the lights on the jets rumbling down
to O'Hare. They carried men wearing ties who drank whiskey sours from
plastic glasses and planned how to get back at people they hated.

As usual I hid my bike by the school across the street and watched his
place for a minute. It looked at first like Hooknose was gone, but when
I let myself in the garage there sat his nerdmobile truck, still bright and
new with that nice showroom smell. In the dark the chrome shined like
an alderman's limo, and I thought of how I'd like to do some little thing
to that truck. Make a tiny scratch in the fender maybe. I could use a nail.
I was feeling around on the workbench when I heard footsteps clomping
from the house.

I done a dive under the bench so quick the hide scraped off the back
of my neck. Light flowed from the kitchen and then from the cab when
Hooknose opened the truck door. At first the cold from the concrete felt
good on my skin. But I ended up with my face jammed next to a can
of gas, and thought I'd choke to death before Hooknose finally found what
he wanted and went back in the house so I could crawl out.

The door leading to the house needed work. I put my ear to it, and
scraped off paint chips with my thumbnail while I listened. There was
no doubt about what was going on in the house. Sex was happening. Sex
has sounds that are as true to it as notes to a song. Sex has its own feel.
Sex takes over a whole house. It's like paint that way. You'll notice paint
first. It's the main thing about a room, the paint. So is sex. It can overcome paint.

Oh, but it's hurtful to think your loved one's having sex with another.
It can make a scrape on the back of your neck seem like a kiss. You wonder
if your partner says the same things and makes the same sounds. But you
can't know. Your loved one won't tell the truth. Your loved one will tell
you that you're the favorite, but such isn't what you want to hear. You
want to know why. The details are what you want to know. I puzzled
about the details. I put my ear back to the door. I peeled off more paint,
and heard more sounds of sex. It should have been enough for me, but
it wasn't.

I opened the can of gas and poured it on the Warshawsky seat covers of Hooknose's truck. It wouldn't soak in so I splashed more over the dashboard where it could run down the defroster wells to the engine. What was left I emptied on the floor mats. I made a fuse of a lit cigarette in a matchbook and I put it on the seat. Then I opened the door to the house, just a crack.

There was no carpet on the hall floor so I stepped carefully, but I didn't need to. I could have arrived on the Jackson Park subway and they wouldn't of looked up. When I got to the bedroom I peeked in just far enough to see the edge of the bed. A radio and a big glass ash tray sat on the nightstand. I took another step and there was Hooknose's naked back, propped up on his arms, red from the sleeve line down where he forgot to put on sunscreen.

I never had what you'd call a *plan*. I just wanted to see Aggie's face when she found out she never had me fooled. I took two steps into the room and yanked the sheet hard as I could. But what I saw under Hooknose's flabby body when he jerked around was not Aggie with her mouth open and her legs spread. It was Louise.

I figured I had just enough time to get back to the garage. But I had hold of the sheet and Louise was yanking it the other way trying to cover all her parts. Hooknose flopped there on his side with his cheeks bulging and his forehead turning pink, and all the while Louise was screaming at me to let go a the goddamn sheet.

You may think that when a matchbook fuse lights a gasoline bomb you hear an explosion. That's not so. The sound it makes is more of a *whump*, like a fat man collapsing on your roof. A whump is what I heard. Oh, there was an explosion, but it was not from the gasoline. It was when Hooknose hit me with the ash tray. That was the crash that followed the whump.

We could of all burned up. They were involved in sex. I was the one with normal wits. Hooknose hit me in the face with that ash tray, and because of it he's a filthy snakeshit in my book. I could of been knocked cold. Instead I started tasting that peach, and then I threw up on Hooknose's bed. Right there on the bed where he'd been having sex with a woman I thought was Aggie.

I'm not a negative person. I tell these apprentices in the barracks there are things I care about. I like beer nuts. I'd swim the Calumet to see

Montgomery Clift. I like that old record of Feliciano singing about all the things Miss Otis Regrets. She was a sad lady too. I like those cannoli with cream cheese. You can't get them here in Greenland. Right off, I figured nobody's gonna hardass me this time. You see, I remembered a couple things from before, like where they keep the gas.

But stuff changes. The third week I'm here the foreman comes up behind me and says, "We ain't paying you to drink coffee."

I look at the clawhammer laying against the ladder and for a second there I think about it. But I take my brush and go back to painting over the pictures, up and down, up and down, smoothing the streaks. The more I moved that brush and thought about the nylon hairs filling in the pores and smooshing out the rot so the wood can live longer, the better I felt. And I painted harder, and I finished the whole wall without ever checking for the foreman even once, and for the first time since my old man was cutting hair in his little shop on Armitage with its sweet smell of Lucky Tiger tonic, I felt at peace.

Aggie, she got a dose of the agreeables and now she's writing me letters, says we'll leave bygones be bygones. Louise and Hooknose Howard got married with the insurance money, she says, and moved to Phoenix and that's good news too. So I went ahead and wrote her back and said everything's okay by me. Another six months I have a nice bundle of earnings and according to the probation court I do what I want. Got a piece of paper says so.

They built a chapel here now, a real one—made of concrete if you can believe it. Them that want to go in are welcome, there's no law or nothing. Me, I walk in now and then. I look at Jesus on a cross they got hanging over the altar. He's got a kind face, Jesus. People that don't see that in him, they're the ones got troubles. Maybe it's time they look at Jesus the way the rest of us do, the way my old man would, the way me and Aggie plan to—the way he looked that time before I touched him with the paint.

Seeing a Cardinal

THEY ARRIVED after supper, Dad behind the wheel of the Chrysler, smiling and straining to push the door open, my mother strapped in like a test pilot. "Well, we made it," Dad said, as I knew he would.

With Susan hovering behind me nervous as a bird, I shook Dad's hand, quick and firm, the way he likes, and gave my mother a careful hug, picking up the lanolin smell in her hair. It would be our only physical contact until parting.

We don't know how to interact, so we all pretend we're glad to be together, and that everything won't go wrong. We begin and end visits with stiff embraces—the way you hug someone who's HIV positive. In between we mind carefully our rule of conversation: Keep it trivial. Near the end we shake our heads and carry on about where the time went, the distance separating us, and how it would be nice to visit more often.

Dad has a number of unfulfilled wishes (a number that grows with his age), among which are to visit the Empire State Building, to see Ozzie Smith in a spring training game, and to observe a cardinal in the wild.

I know the last doesn't rank with the other two, but my father, who will be seventy-nine in December, claims to have never seen a cardinal, and knows of the bird's existence only as the symbol of his favorite baseball team. It may be true that he's never spotted one, for he's not an attentive person. Nor is he lucky. He buys when the market screams to sell, takes

71

the bow seat of the boat while fish slide by the stern, and wanders toward the restroom as home runs are about to be struck.

There are no cardinals where my family comes from. In that cool country live robins, sparrows, barnswallows, and hordes of fidgety, irritating small-beaked birds that leave their droppings on windshields where they freeze into speckled rings hard enough to break an ice scraper.

I love spending money when I'm down. Last winter I took a trip back east with my father. We were over Ohio when we got the news about skyscrapers blowing up in New York. Dad insisted we had nothing to worry about, but I talked him into taking the first flight south we could get. In St. Petersburg we rented a car and drove to Al Lang Field where the Cards train, arriving in time to watch the ground crew hauling down the flags and covering the field before the five-day storm hit. We stood shivering at the wire gates, trying to see in. "I sure expected it to be greener," said Dad.

"Look!" I said. It was Ozzie Smith, not ten feet away, standing at the curb with the collar of his camel-hair coat pulled up around his neck. Dad looked not where I was pointing, but toward a man hammering plywood over the concession stand window. By the time I got him turned around, Ozzie had hopped into his limo and was out of sight.

It's inconvenient to have company just now. Beatrice, who will become my ex-wife when the court grinds through its depressing load of words and paper, lives across two streets and three houses down, in the green two-bedroom she and I owned for four months. We were both supposed to leave, but Bea worked out something with the realtor. Several weeks ago I wandered down our old alley thinking to snatch back the bird feeder I'd forgotten in the haste of moving. I knocked on the back door, just to check how Bea had been holding up. She was crying.

"What is it?" I asked, not quite ready to believe it had to do with the sight of me.

But it was. "You look so *delicate*," she said. "And afraid. Coming through the gate, you looked like you thought somebody was going to bite you." Then she blew her nose into the wadded Kleenex she keeps in her sleeve. "The other thing is I gained four pounds."

I told her I couldn't imagine where those pounds were. I put one arm around her shoulder, resting my thumb on the knob of a bone that seems missing in Susan, and one thing led to another.

Susan, who I met when she found me in the library reading room asleep under the newspaper, and made of me a project—allowing me step-by-step into her car, her confidence, her kitchen, and her bedroom—knows nothing of my contact with Bea and thinks the divorce is imminent. My parents share the belief.

It was Susan's idea to invite them here. She thought the structure of a visit would be good for me. It was true my days had become loose. At first I went to twelve-step meetings and registered for a computer course at the college. I got a job interview even—for electronic petitioning, they called it. I was slow in understanding they wanted me to talk people into signing up for burial insurance. I'd work at a desk, with a dialing machine so I wouldn't actually have to look my customer in the eye like a mortician over a casket. But they never called me back. The computer course was a joke—the teacher expected us to do *every*thing, rather than the other way around. And after that Susan's project stalled. I got her to put in cable, and instead of playing Scrabble and talking until midnight like we used to, she began going to bed after Letterman's monologue while I watched Victor Mature movies on AMC. I started sleeping later, listening for her hair dryer, the rattle of the newspaper—all the fading sounds of her morning departure—before getting up, not wanting to realize the only thing on my schedule was walking over to see Bea twice a week.

"And three years is much too long," insisted Susan. I think she secretly wanted to meet my parents so she can grill them about me, find out what makes me tick. My mother and father know about Susan through my brother who earlier took care of the touchy business of telling them about the split with Bea. I think they're pleasantly surprised. I can imagine what they expected. But Susan is educated and polite. A real find actually, considering. My niece says she's much too nice for this family.

Dad picked at Susan's rhubarb pie, leaving part of the crust. His attention was on the bird feeder.

Cardinals had been visiting the feeder all spring. I loaded it with sunflower seeds, honey, and cracked corn. Ordinarily we'd see a cardinal three or four times a day along with swarms of hatches and chickadees crowding the perches like boys waiting for a parade.

"You'll have to be quick," I said.

"I don't guess you saw cardinals in Canada either," said Dad.

"They wouldn't have them that far north," said my mother.

Dad gave a little jerk with his chin. My mother missed it. "He wasn't there to birdwatch."

"I never paid much attention," I said, wanting to be peacemaker.

"You mean they do have them in Canada, too?" asked my mother.

Dad put his fork down. "I know they don't. That isn't what I'm talking about."

My mother frowned, looking for a way to help Dad save face. Susan was stepping carefully toward the sink, dishes tottering in her hands. "He wasn't in Canada that long anyway," said my mother.

"There you go again," said Dad, folding his arms. "He couldn't have seen them if they're not there. So the hell with it then."

Later I watched Susan measuring careful tablespoons of coffee into a paper filter, feeling a flush of warmth, pleased with myself for having warned her. She was new to these family secrets. "See what I'm talking about?" I said.

She shook her head. "It was a simple misunderstanding. Don't be so ready to give up."

With Susan at work and my parents napping I hurried across Division and Clark, then down the alley, past weed piles, broken appliances, and all the other minor household embarrassments that people slide to the background like diseased relatives. Two beagles growled at me through a flimsy fence. Ants were crawling over mulberries squashed on the road. I cut left through the garage, spotting the shelves I built, crossed the too-big yard with its moldy, dry smell of the leaves I neglected to rake, and stepped into Bea's kitchen. I thought I heard a door close, but Bea was at the sink, spraying cool water over her wrists. She'd just finished a workout and perspiration glistened on the back of her neck.

I tugged at her waist band, but she turned her hip into the counter. "Was somebody here?" I asked. "I heard a voice."

"No," she said. "Just Richard."

"Richard?"

"Honestly, you're so *dense*. Richard Simmons, on the TV." She dried her hands on a towel crocheted with figures of smiling cooks, their fat fists clutching rolling pins. It was a wedding present from my grandmother.

I said, "Well, they made it."

"Grand. Are they asking about me?"

"They wonder how you are," I lied.

"I guess we're still married in their eyes," Bea said, making a mark on my Sierra Club calendar under the day's date.

"Until we sign the rest of the papers."

She studied the calendar, flipping the leaves. "We could save money if we held up the paperwork. Which we probably should think about."

This was out of the blue. Bea had changed, she was never so decisive. "Well, there is Susan," I said.

"Yes, your little lady, only she's not so little, is she?"

This was the old Bea. She hadn't changed *that* much.

"She takes thyroid pills. You should see, she eats like a bird." I felt further compelled to defend Susan, so I added, "Looks aren't everything."

Bea studied me, calculating. "Good thing for her. Anyway, Rafe says there's a chance on getting the house back. His buyer is pulling in chips, wants assets more liquid considering the cost of money. With so little equity it might work out."

"Rafe?"

Bea giggled. "Rafael, the realtor."

"That slimy bastard's still around?"

Now things were making sense. Two years ago Beatrice hadn't known liquid assets and equity from cheese sauce and fettucine. But my remark brought her around, jerking her out of her coyness. "He was a lifesaver, and you know very well he's married, happily. The thing about you is that you're weak. Why don't you just tell that poor girl you're having other thoughts? After all, she's going to throw you out some day anyway."

Because it's been so long since my mother's voice awakened me, I at first couldn't make any sense of it. She spoke carefully, not wanting to come into the bedroom occupied by her married son and his girlfriend.

"Dad's sick," she was saying.

He'd stayed up to watch the Cards game from the West Coast, and now he lay back on the recliner, maroon pajamas buttoned, gray hair matted, eyes closed.

I leaned over him. "What is it?"

He opened his eyes and drew a short, sharp breath. "My goddamn back seized up on me," he said. "I can't get out of this chair and now I got cramps." He pried his pajamas open with a thumb, groaning softly with the effort.

What was I expected to do? I was certain paramedics don't tend to locked backs. I tried to think. He grunted with each exhalation, as if pushing his breath past an obstruction.

"How do you normally take care of this?"

It took him a minute. "Usually it goes away by itself." He was using his fingers like a probe, working on his spine and around to his abdomen.

"Have you had a bowel movement?" A desperate question, but the problem resided in the general area.

He looked at my mother who was hovering behind me.

"Not since we left," she said.

"Maybe a hot water bottle would relax the muscles."

He thought about it. "Maybe," he said. I ran to find the bottle. Together we lowered the chair and got him turned over. In the process his pajama bottoms slid down past one hip.

After that there was nothing for me but to sit holding the bottle where he said it felt best, and wait. I studied him. My brother has his angular face. I have the hands—long fingers with blunt tips. How curious, what age does. The protruding chin, knees, hips—all the bones rounded and enlarged. But as the bones grow the flesh diminishes until the skin hangs, humbled and tired.

My father's upper body remained large through the shoulders, his arms strong and nicely formed. But his legs had withered until they seemed scarcely able to support the thickened middle. He shifted to his side, grunting. Does pubic hair turn gray? No, at least not on my father. The penis— object of immense and unending curiosity from my childhood. Standing at urinals, peeing in the ditch with the car as a shield. Checking out the corner of my eye, wondering: Will mine get as big as his? I still don't think it is. Confronting my existence. I'm an accident.

Mild cramps replaced his steady pain. He lay there staring upward, his corneas opaque, the glacier-blue of age. He twisted about, creating sounds of stress from deep within the recliner. During the worst of these spasms his mouth skewed inward, as if to speak. *Is this the best you can do?* I expected him to say.

Instead, he asked what the score was. I had no idea. My mother had lowered the volume. "Cards are ahead," I said.

I went to refill the bottle with warmer water, and Susan motioned me into the bedroom. "I learned a good relaxation technique in yoga," she said.

"*Yoga?* Forget it. He hates that stuff."

"All right. But I'll show you just in case."

When I got back he was sitting up, white-faced. "I need the bathroom quick," he said.

I told him to lower his head until it touched his chest. Then I raised his arms slowly toward the ceiling. "*Oh,*" he said. "Oh boy. *That's* better."

"It was my pie, wasn't it?" Susan said as I got back into bed.

According to Audubon, cardinals are of the grosbeak family, they are distinguished from scarlet tanagers by their black faces and their crests, and they visit feeders regularly. When most people envision cardinals they are seeing the males. To human eyes the females are gray and drab.

Although the family won't mention the incident again—better a world of pain than a single embarrassment—my father behaved as if his back spasms had earned the right to enjoy coddling even beyond his normal excess. Susan phoned the clinic dietician to ask what foods would help, and picked up three kinds of laxatives and two pain relievers at the drugstore. She busied herself setting up the footstool, shopping for the chocolate drops he loves, worrying over him with pillows and cushions.

Dad has always expected others to attend to him. My brother trots about like a manservant, bringing toothpicks, reading glasses, the sports section. Dad will hold out his empty glass, waving it like a drunk signaling the bartender, until someone sweeps by and returns it filled with water.

I asked Susan, "Am I like that? Do I expect you to wait on me?"

She turned the light out. "It's different with us," she said.

"Then I do?"

I could sense her deliberating in the dark, weighing the options. "I think you're careful around me because you don't think of this place as your home yet," she said, not really answering.

"You pay the rent."

She quietly summoned her patience. We'd had this conversation before. "I'd pay it if you weren't here. I care for you."

"Well, was I right about him?"

"You exaggerated. He's a gentle old man who loves to talk. That must be where you get it. If only he'd stop calling me 'Bea.'"

The following morning brought what I suspected was the real reason my parents came so far—the opportunity for a reunion with Dad's old business partner who's retired to little place southeast of here. I last saw the man when I was about eight years old, and now I went along out of expectations I'd know the way.

When we pulled into his driveway Jake jogged out and threw his arms around Dad. I'd seen that so much growing up. People clapping him on the back, asking after his health, loving him. And each time I'd think: If only they knew.

Jake and Dad reminisced about the old days when they were in the rag business, as they called it. They talked of lady's slacks, how if you want to sell your extra small and extra large, you have to have a lot of mediums. Customers like to think they have a wide choice, even if the choice means nothing. They talked about fabrics, and the styles, types and colors that wouldn't sell. Burgundy for instance. It sounds elegant to me. But it had little demand among farm families in the great Midwest.

"Say, do you get cardinals around here?" asked Dad.

"Sure," said Jake. "I saw one in the cottonwood this morning. You keep checking out there you'll see him. It's the boys that are red, you know."

We were in New Madrid, Missouri, where a hundred and fifty years ago an earthquake struck with such power that it stopped the flow of the Mississippi. Dad asked Jake what he knew about it, and he took us to a farm outside town which was the center of where the thing hit. We stopped the car to look. The field appeared like any other, with bi-leaved corn plants sprouting in the soft black soil, and granaries in need of paint. I tried to imagine what it must have been like when it happened. But my speculations took me nowhere. Almost no one lived there then and who's to tell about the wild animals?

I did the driving home through a heavy rain. A truck blared past, isolating us in sheets of water. The road curved, then curved again, and I got lost. "Don't worry," Dad said. "We'll find the way." Then he put his head back on the seat and fell asleep. When I couldn't see the fine, white curls of my mother's hair in the mirror I knew she'd stretched out on the back seat. I kept driving, through the black night, trying to make out signs while the windshield wipers squeaked and the rain fell in streams.

Dad woke once to ask my mother for the pillow. He always gets the pillow, just as he always gets the largest piece of fudge cake, the tastiest end of the pork roast, the fullest glass of lemonade—the warmest, the driest, the first, the last, the biggest, the best.

He stirred again only as we turned onto Division Street. He checked his watch and looked at the house, blinking. "Well, we made it," he said.

Sex comes natural between former partners. You've overcome the fragile barriers that hold the world in a sexual check. You don't have to pretend anymore, or fear rejection. A refusal has long since lost its sting.

I felt awful about resuming sex with Bea. Susan knows she lives close by, but never asks about her. Maybe it wouldn't have happened if it weren't so efficient. Even in sex we avoid the inconvenience.

"I think I'd miss your father most," Bea said. We were on the living room carpet with its faint, new-car smell. Bea won't allow me in our old bed— she insists on making love only in fresh places, like the hallway or attic.

"I thought you considered him spoiled."

She folded her hands behind her head. "I never said that, even if he is. The thing about him is that he always notices me, if I have my hair done, what earrings I have on. Quick, close your eyes and tell me what I'm wearing." Her hand flew to cover my sight.

"You're wearing nothing."

I could have told her what she *had* been wearing—the same pair of blue sweats she'd worn for a month. She'd gained weight, I could see it, and she dared to talk about Susan.

"You get that precision from your mother, always having to be correct. I miss her too, though. Maybe I could have them over."

"You're not serious."

"Why not? See if they'll come for coffee, I'd love to talk to your dad. I could have some news. Or maybe I'll just call."

I sat up. The carpet was scratchy. I'd picked it for its price. Bea said it looked like gray astroturf. "If you call, try during the day when Susan's at work. I got to go. They'll be waking up."

Bea raised herself up on her elbows. "Don't you want to know what news I have?"

"Sure." I assumed she intended to bring them in on all the hints she'd been dropping about getting back together.

"Remember how we tried and tried and tried to have a baby?"

"The expensive pills and the counting, yes."

"Well," she sang. "Guess what?"

Dad can't eat whole grains, lactose, or Vitamin C. I'm not certain why, unless it's to add to the already stupendous volume of concerns for his health forced on those surrounding him. My mother says Vitamin C alters the acid in the blood, and grains lodge in the pockets of his intestines, causing infection. Then we encounter familiar rounds of antibiotics, liquid diets, and bowel-movement monitoring.

My mother is the whole grain checker. She scrapes the tops of buns, smashes vegetables with the back of a spoon, examines desserts like a burglar going over last night's haul.

"Oh shucks. Daddy better not eat this," she said to Susan. It was raspberry shortcake. It came from a mix so whatever distant relationship the stuff had to real raspberries had certainly been boiled and beat out of it between the raspberry bush and the colorful cardboard box. I told my mother as much.

"I don't want to hurt feelings," she said. "But you just can't tell for sure."

That meant no one else could have raspberry shortcake either. Susan whisked it away, much too cheerfully I thought. Then we got into a discussion on whether corn-on-the-cob contains lactose or grains.

"Of course it has grains," my mother said. "That's what corn is. Grain."

"I realize that," I said. "But that can't be what they mean. It's only a grain on a technicality. If something that size can hurt him there must be a lot of other things you don't even know about."

Again Susan intervened. "I don't like corn anyway," she said. "Let's have those microwave carrots."

"Thank you Sue," my mother said. "No sense in taking a chance after all we've been through."

I dropped my parents at the mall and went to keep my appointment at the clinic with the fertility specialist. This would have surprised Bea—she always wanted me to go. They showed me into a cubicle, handed me a small, gray plastic cup, and told me to masturbate.

"Take your time," the attendant said, as if I were there to pick out a pocket watch.

I sat for a while, feeling the vibrating footsteps on the carpeted floor of the broad hallway. Back and forth they went, technicians, nurses, people with ruined lungs, miserable blood, crushed bones. I opened the drawer in the little metal table. Inside was a chart demonstrating the correct way to fasten the straps on disposable gowns. Beneath it was a *People* magazine. I folded the magazine open to concentrate on the model in a Tanqueray ad, but she wore a green bathing suit that cast her skin in a ghostly pallor, like the people on MTV. I ran the image of the receptionist through my imagination, but my focus stayed on her braces. After a time I walked out, feeling sensible and smug over this tiny moral victory, leaving the cup behind as unviolated as I found it.

Even as my father sleeps down the hall, grumbling in his dreams, I lie awake skimming over the swamp of the future. I'll become a lovable but selfish tyrant, waited on hand and foot by my melancholy wife (Susan probably, Bea would never tolerate it), a twenty-first century Henry Higgins. The genes must have their way. And my children, the unborn males, grousing toward eternity. Maybe they'll never exist, my sperm being futile fish after all. It's good, the way I abandoned the specimen cup.

At seventy-nine how long can you keep going? Picasso, Irving Berlin, Eubie Blake. What are the prospects? He could leave me anytime. That's the big fear. He might be gone before he gets better, before he gets a chance to say he didn't mean it.

How did he get that way? Maybe it was his war. The great war. Not the Great War, but the great *war*. The war. The one that needs no identification.

War and depression. Depression and the War—the central facts of my father's existence.

I can't imagine conflict among members of my father's generation. I think of them—butchers and bakers, Uncle Ralph and Auntie Liz, all pushing the same buttons on the jukebox, dropping identical dollar bills in the collection plate, believing Eisenhower, hand on the left breast, content in a harmless sort of way, as if they'd materialized from one of my Victor Mature movies where people are shot and die but show neither bullet hole nor blood.

Fifties adults were always smiling—rouge-faced, wavy hair. Bea would fit right in. The war was over and they'd survived, won it, beat Hitler and Tojo, and there was enough butter and gasoline. Was it so hard for them? Did he really do all of that for me—go to war, work sixty hours a week, get by without a car. Did he have me in mind? I'd like to ask him if those were the best years of his life. But I won't. Maybe I'll ask my mother.

We sat on the porch the evening before they left, Dad in the big recliner, me on one of those weightless lawn chairs that fold up under you when you stand.

"I thought you said there were cardinals here."

I expected that. "You must be scaring them off," I said, hating all birds at that moment.

I know he's loved back home. In the den there's a cardboard box full of certificates and plaques—there's even a photo of the governor shaking his hand. Everyone knows him. It takes a long time to go to the post office with Dad. Walking behind him you meet the smiles of people left in his wake.

He could have argued, if he were an arguer of God, man and nature, rather than of who left the garage door open, that his hard work allowed me to prepare for life. I had friends who married young, produced a family, and insisted they didn't have time to protest. They were too occupied with ear infections and Enfamil.

Dad cared only for his back yard. He knew what he wanted to know. And for that I hated him, though I should love him all the more—for he took very good care of his yard, and of his family, and of me. He was just wise enough to know who and what he could care for, and weigh it against how hard he could work. And so he cast his Republican vote faithfully every two years, and hoped for the best.

"You're at the point where you better show some backbone," Bea said, when I phoned to tell her we were running out of time.

I pointed out to her that at least I'd made the call. I could have done nothing and simply allowed them to return home. Then I tried to explain to her that I thought we should put things on hold for a while, and how I was a wreck from all that time with my parents.

"You mean you'd leave me in this situation?" she said.

"If you're talking about being pregnant I don't think I had anything to do with it. You remember, they said my sperm were attenuated or something. And Susan and I haven't used— "

Her voice turned hard as she interrupted. "I don't care to hear about your sex life with that fat bitch!"

I could imagine her there by my calendar, each pale square marked with a penciled check, counting off the days. "Bea," I said. "Would you mind too much if I took the bird feeder that's still in the back yard?"

"You son-of-a-bitch," she said. "You *are* just like your asshole father. One and the same. Self-centered pricks. You'll be sorry sooner than you think."

Susan worked hard on eggs Benedict for the going-away breakfast. Dad spent an hour in the bathroom, and when he got to the table his breakfast was cold. He picked at the cinnamon roll and afterward made straight for my mother's travel bag where he knew he'd find Hershey bars.

While Susan worried over her sauces and pans my mother and I sat on the porch, watching the birds in the evergreens. This was to be our conversation, the single one we'd share this year. I studied her sitting there, smiling politely, her boney hands palm up on her lap as if ready to receive a large load of clean towels.

"What would you do different in your life if you had a second chance?" I asked.

My mother blushed. She long ago learned how to divert serious dialogue. "Do different?" she said, as if the phrase had no meaning in this language. "Nothing, I guess." She turned stiffly and looked toward the kitchen. "Susan must need help."

"She's doing fine. You know I've been wondering. What were things like when I was small? What did you do for fun?"

My mother is slightly hard of hearing. If she doesn't catch what you're saying she pitches her face forward, expectantly, smiling, as if what she's missed is sure to be cheerful.

"Fun? You forget we had the county fair and church suppers."

"No, not that. How did you get through the *tedious* part of life. Dad worked six days a week, and I remember you had a job for a while."

"People entertained themselves."

"How?"

She paused to think. Her face became dreamy. Apparently she remembered it as a good time. The past gets filtered. Family histories should be written day to day. "Well, we had radio. Back then it was better than TV. I don't care what they say. Your Auntie Liz was a great comfort, a great help."

"What do you mean by comfort? During the war?"

"No, later. When you boys were in diapers, those years." She looked back over her shoulder. "Liz and I stayed home playing rummy, but don't think your father didn't know how to have a good time."

This pleased me, the idea of my uptight father enjoying himself. "You mean out with the fellas?"

My mother leaned forward. "I suppose so. We never asked."

Susan brought a jar of jelly for me to open. "I better get Dad out of the bathroom," said my mother. But she made no move to go.

"You should be thankful of one thing," she said, when Susan was gone.

"What's that?"

"Two things really. That you have Susan—she's good for you. And that you and Bea never had children. You should be very thankful."

Her face, momentarily grave, returned to its crinkly sparkle. She'd come safely back from the worrisome trip to the ancient past. She smiled softly and I knew that was all I was going to get. She rocked back on the recliner and folded her hands, her chin bobbing gently.

Half an hour before they were to leave Dad decided the wiper blades looked bad. He'd spotted replacements in Target for only three-fifty. I fumbled with them while he watched. For some reason the old blade wouldn't come off. I twisted and tugged on the end but it wouldn't budge. I was ready to cut it with the pinking shears when he reached past me with those hands so much like my own, did something to the wiper that made a click, and pulled the old one off. "There you go," he said.

He watched, ready to step in again, as I wedged the fresh blades in place.

"Remember your old Plymouth?"

"Yeah."

Whenever anything to do with vehicles comes up he mentions the old Plymouth, my first car. He'll never let me forget what I did to the engine.

"Whatever happened to that car?"

"It had that oil leak. Remember?"

"Oh that's right."

Why won't he talk to me like Bea does? I thought. Call me a name. Tell me to make up my mind. Shape up. Or at least communicate like my mother – hint at something. Give me a lead. Show me he feels, cares, hurts, thinks. Isn't he at all puzzled that I seem to have nowhere to go during the day? Why doesn't he ask about my job prospects, my crumbled marriage, my relationship to Susan? Don't they wonder where I'm going and if I'm ever going to get there?

"So how's Bea?" he asked, jiggling the wiper blade, testing it.

"Fine I guess. I don't see her anymore much."

"Things can haunt a person," he said. "Best to cut it off just like that." He made a karate gesture with his hand.

"Yeah," I said. "And how are you feeling in general?"

"Fine, real swell. And you?"

"Pretty good."

We leaned against the car like two old friends, passing a summer day in the sun.

"Your mother figures I'm not so good," he said, lowering his voice though she was nowhere in sight. "She thinks I got a foot in the grave and the other on a banana peel."

"Yeah?"

"Oh yes, but I'm going to fool her. I might live twenty years."

"Oh, you will for sure," I said.

Impending movement always excited him. His eyes twinkled in the morning brightness. And he was pleased with himself, pleased that he'd always been able to fool my mother.

"After all, it might be that long before I see a cardinal."

At last they were ready, their suitcases arranged just so in the trunk, Susan's carefully-wrapped sandwiches on the back seat, Dad finished fussing with his seat belt. Smiles, waves, everyone happy. I thought to myself, *You'll make it,* as the Chrysler rolled away on Division Street.

I waited for Susan to bring iced tea. She insists on it. There is love in her hopeful eyes as she hands it to me. She watches my eyes to see if it's being returned. She asks questions with her eyes. *Are you better? Do you love me? Why are you here?* She tells me she loves me and the expression goes to the heart, simple and clear, unlike the message from Bea, whose identical words came thick and complex as a Tolstoy novel, laden with subplots, hidden meanings, demands.

Susan constantly surprises. She knows who Frank Lovejoy and Jimmy Piersall are. She agrees that Peggy Lee singing "Fever" is more erotic than the best Madonna's done yet. She likes the way I arrange my music, with "Ode to Joy" and John Lee Hooker on the same tape, and she cares not at all if fondue and long hair are out of fashion. She spoils me with blueberry pastries and omelettes of startling size and content.

When I see her I see myself. When she's mad at the phone company it's my own implanted anger I'm observing. When I try to calm her I know I'm simply reassuring myself.

I was drained, too tired to drink my tea, but Susan if anything seemed on edge, full of nervous energy that they were finally gone. "So how did you survive my father?"

"He said he liked my cooking, especially the rhubarb pie. He gave me a hug and told me I have old-fashioned ears. He's sweet."

"Why does everyone say that?"

"It's hard for you to see."

"It's impossible. What if I'm like that when I get old?"

Susan slid the paper napkin from under her tea. "Maybe I won't be around."

"Why wouldn't you be?"

"We've never talked about it."

"Since when does it need discussing?"

Susan turned in her chair and dabbed at her eyes. "Since your dad suggested I bring it up."

"He did?"

She worked her fingers through the napkin. "Yeah. And so I am, but not in the way he said."

"What do you mean?"

She sniffed and shrugged. She leaned over to set her glass of tea on the floor. She sniffed again. "I've decided you'll have to leave."

"What do you mean?" I repeated. "Leave?"

"Move out. For a while, permanently maybe. You just have to try harder. I don't *care* if you don't have a job—if you'll just be happy without one."

The sweet, baked-dough aromas of breakfast still hung in the air, heavy around us with reminders of my mother and father. "My parents like you a lot," I said, lamely.

Susan started making balls of the napkin, arranging them in ragged rows on her lap. "I know you've been seeing your wife. I can't say anything. You're still married to her."

I said, "Let's table it for now, okay? I'll fix things. You won't need to worry."

"No," she said. "It's too late. And I never worry."

The ice cubes in her glass shifted with a click. She began crying softly. At that moment I felt I loved her, but I also sensed helplessness. "What is it you want me to do?"

She took a minute to catch her breath. "I don't know. I can't command you or change you. I just wish you were more like your father."

We watched the yard in silence. Finally Susan went inside, closing the screen door behind her, quiet as an angel. Immense bluish thunderheads loomed from the west. Mr. Hassey, a man as old as the town, made his way on the sidewalk, his cane wobbling with each step. I waved through the screen, but Mr. Hassey didn't acknowledge me.

My peripheral vision caught a flash of red, feathers descending, cavorting on the lawn, then fluttering to the diseased elm—I expect they'll pull it down any day. I watched the cardinal for a full five minutes. They are so rich and red, so perfect—so beautiful they don't seem real. No wonder they're so hard to see.

Season for a Son

FOR MY FATHER, FOR MY SON

I HADN'T seen him in four years. I expected to find him changed, stretched out from the soft, smiling kindergartner he'd been.

His mother's letter was full of conditions. She advised me to return him on schedule, cautioned me to meet his flight on time, and even explained how to find the gate. She was reminding me that thanks to her sister up in Evanston, she knew her way around Chicago.

She wanted a phone number for "emergencies." I gave her my landlord's number, not a great idea considering a certain incident over a broken window, but it was all I had. She ended typically: "If you wish future visits with Matt please try to cooperate. I shouldn't have to warn you against pulling something funny."

Pulling something funny. By that she meant violating the divorce agreement that specified visits be solely at the discretion of the custodial parent. Solely at the discretion is how two weeks becomes four years. Four years defended by a single sentence: *All you had to do was ask.*

I was to have a little more than a day with him, and an urgency haunted me. The thought that all might not go well, that the visit might sever our fragile link worried me beyond distraction.

We would devote most of the time to baseball, of course. My passion for it has been lifelong. In baseball I see forms of truth that escape others. They consider my game dull and slow, but I think of their football with its territorial singularity as brutish and demeaning, like Panzers invading the Low Countries.

I'd called for a room at a Holiday Inn on the West side. I knew Matt might think it strange that we not stay in my apartment. It wasn't that I chose to hide things from him—one look at my old Volkswagen would reveal enough about me. I simply felt unprepared to allow him so completely into my world. In my apartment he'd sleep in my bed, sit in my chair. He could study my photos. This would be fine some day. But not yet. For the moment we'd settle for a motel room, clean and neutral.

"Hey, Pal!" I called my old greeting.

He looked at me as if he were staring into a window. "Hi," he said. He was chewing on a wad of pink gum.

I meant to greet him with a hug, but he was so changed from the round bundle I'd known that I hesitated. I reached for him but the handle on his bag got tangled in his fingers. A woman with a guitar shoved us out of the traffic lane.

"You look different," he said. "Where's your beard?" He would remember. My beard had gone with the marriage.

We moved outside. The crowd thinned. I lit a cigarette. "Oh, you still smoke," he said, and he wrinkled his nose.

"Afraid so." With a comic gesture, I held the pack toward him. "Want one?" He stared at it.

"No thanks," he said. "I got asthma so I can't be around smoke."

I dropped the cigarette on the concrete. "Oh, it's okay outside," he said. "But Mom says I should tell you not to smoke in the car." He pried the gum from his mouth and plunked it in the center of a trash barrel by the curb.

At the parking lot he stopped in front of a long tan car. He stood for a moment studying it. "This is like the one my dad's gonna get."

I slid another cigarette out of the pack in my shirt pocket. My lighter refused to work. I smacked it on the flat of my hand.

"I mean my step-dad, you're my dad," he said. "Bruce. You know, Mom's new husband."

"I know who you mean." My lighter caught. The flame radiated hot against the tip of my nose. "Do you call him 'Dad'?"

"No—well, once in a while. Him and Mom told me it's okay if I want to. Anyhow, he's gonna buy a Maserati, just like this one." Matt circled the car. I waited, smoking my cigarette until he was ready.

He seemed distracted on the way to the motel. I guess he was insecure.
"Say, Pal," I said. "You know the Cubs are only three out?"

He stared in fascination at the stream of vehicles in the adjoining lane.
The VW whined as we pulled around a truck full of lazy-eyed cattle. I
wasn't sure if he heard me. Just then a sleek, white arrow of a car streaked
past us.

"Wow, look at that." He pushed himself up on the seat, his eyes bright.
"It must be an Avanti."

"Did you hear me?" I said. He turned to me. The Avanti had moved
ahead and out of sight.

"What did you say?"

"I got tickets for the game this afternoon."

"You mean baseball game?"

"Yeah, the Cubs. Is that okay with you?"

"Sure," he said, slumping back on the seat. "I just don't connect with
baseball much. Bruce says it's boring."

So this was my son. The one person in the world I could pass my values
on to. He had inherited half his genes from me, and therefore should share
my tendencies, maybe even my beliefs. Perhaps he needed encouragement.
But society with its tedious maxims said that I had forfeited the right to
provide that encouragement. I had the privilege at my son's birth, but gave
it up when I became divorced.

I suppose divorce implies a kind of choice as does marriage. The pro-
found truth settling on me held that I would rather be without my son
than be with his mother—though I'd never thought of it exactly in those
terms. I wondered if he had.

The clerk at the registration desk couldn't find my name on his reserva-
tions list. We waited several minutes, and I felt a familiar surge of temper.
I watched the clerk. His pale throat seemed inadequate.

"When did you phone, sir?"

"I told you, last week."

"But what day?"

"I don't know, Tuesday probably."

Matt leaned against me. I wished he'd go check the sports cars in the
parking lot.

"I'm sorry, it just doesn't seem to be here."

The clerk called his superior who studied the same list and asked the same questions. He offered to put us in a different room, one closer to the pool—but more expensive.

"How much?" I asked.

The price was nearly double. I could barely afford the regular room.

"You do take checks?"

"Yes sir. Of course they must be secured by a credit card."

"What does that mean?" My voice rose, too quickly. Matt looked at me.

The clerk explained that policy required them to hold my credit card number on file in case the check failed to clear.

"So what the hell's the difference? I might as well use my card—right?" Matt was toying with the call bell on the counter.

"Whatever you prefer, sir."

The clerk's politeness angered me more. Matt rang the call bell softly. The clerk smiled at him. I worked my Visa out of my wallet and flipped it on the counter. The clerk nodded and disappeared into the office.

I looked at Matt. "What do you think, Pal?"

"Maybe we should stay at your house," he said.

A shade of reason to his voice gave me pause, but only for a second. "No," I said. "We'll be fine." Just then the clerk came out of the office.

"I'm sorry, sir. Your card was not approved for that amount."

"Not approved—what do you mean?"

"They say that according to their records your balance has exceeded your limit." He handed me the card.

I stared at him, barely aware of Matt hovering by my elbow.

"Well kiss my ass, you pasty little son-of-a-bitch," I said.

Someone walked toward us, the manager, I guessed. I'd have grabbed his collar, but we were on the way out. There was a free standing ash tray just inside the door. I turned and gave it a kick. White sand and ashes billowed on to the carpet. The manager danced out of the way, his polished black shoes shining like coins in the artificial light.

We found a room in a motel off Dempster. The swimming pool was closed—for cleaning, they said. A sign on the door ordered us: TURN AIR

Conditioner To Low Or Off When Leaving. The room was stuffy, and the window when opened brought traffic noise from the street. But we didn't mind. We hardly needed the room except for sleep. In fact it was time already to leave for the stadium.

Matt had said little after we left the Holiday Inn. For the first time I realized that I wasn't alone in gathering impressions. I wondered if he saw me as a picture of his time to come—as if he were trapped in a genetic lock. Maybe he felt doomed to perpetual denial with sons he'd never know. I resolved to adjust my behavior. The visit had just begun, and with care I could overcome the bad notions he'd formed.

"Well, Pal, ready to head out?"

He was watching television and didn't respond. I repeated myself. He turned the TV off, stepped into the bathroom and closed the door.

I wanted to get going. I needed the easy familiarity of the stadium. I longed to talk baseball. I turned the TV on to check the weather forecast. The harsh noise and image of an auto race leaped at me. Just then Matt came out of the bathroom.

"Hey, I didn't know you liked NASCAR," he said.

I should have been pleased. At last he expressed interest in something other than exotic cars with unpronounceable names. But unfortunately I considered auto racing as the cultural equivalent of football—which is to say it fell in the domain of beer-guzzling nincompoops.

"Well," I said. "I do follow the Indianapolis 500."

Matt returned to the bathroom.

"I like horse racing, too," I called through the door. "Maybe we can go to the track some time."

"Sure," he yelled back. Then he opened the door and looked at me for a long moment. "Should we go now?" he said.

Wrigley Field sits like a quaint museum, lovingly tended to, zealously preserved, a green refuge in a sea of asphalt and glass. Here seven decades of Aprils have instilled joy in the young and youth in the old. The mortar in the center field bricks had barely dried when doughboys marched up gangplanks to ships bound for France. Their sons hiked to war also, and then their sons. Other sons found other wars and some who marched away never returned. But the game was still played at Wrigley.

Even in winter it inspires gladness. I first saw it through the window of the elevated train on a dark December morning. I'd arrived in Chicago days before, newly divorced, with no job and few prospects. The sign appeared first, then the gray dormancy of the stadium itself. It rested there in the snow and ice just as it always had, promising warm days and better times.

Spring arrived. Outfield seats were two dollars then, and I saw a dozen games before the season was a month old. The first was a pitcher's nightmare, won with a Cub homer in the tenth inning, and in three hours thirty years of Dodger devotion melted away like a Sno-Cone in the bleacher sun. At once I knew what Franklin Adams felt when he wrote the verse that haunts the truest fan.

> "These are the saddest of all possible words,
> Tinker to Evers to Chance . . ."

They were quick as cats and they turned double plays that were the joy of bellowing stockyard workers with beery grins and cloth caps. At home the moments were replayed for wide-eyed children who passed them on to their children. Stories going back to the nineteenth century. Of Cap Anson. A man so agile he never was hit by a pitch. Of Kiki Cuyler. And Ernie Banks. Fathers and sons. And now it was my turn.

I squeezed into a parking spot behind a van from Iowa. When I got out to check whether I was over the yellow line, the engine on the VW started sputtering as if diseased. Matt stretched his foot across the floor board and revved it to life.

As we approached the stadium a white car captured his attention. He said it was a Lamborghini, and he raved about it. I became frustrated trying to explain how Greg Maddux would pitch to the Braves, but I let it go. Wrigley Field has transformed into a fan many a person who didn't know a baseball from a bassoon.

We found our seats on the first base side, twenty rows back — good foul ball territory. Although I'd come close, I'd never caught a ball. What a day it would make, I thought, if I could offer Matt a baseball rubbed up by Maddux or fouled off by Ryne Sandberg. I wasn't sure I could part with such a treasure, even as a gift to my son.

The good ballpark smell of strong mustard and steamy hot dogs reached us. The vendor followed. The stands filled. Hardly a place remained vacant.

I began writing in my scorecard during the lull that followed batting practice. I'm fond of this ballpark moment. An air of invigoration descends, equivalent to the sounds musicians produce when they tune their instruments before a performance — a prelude of chaos necessary for an event of beauty.

Two or three players ran wind sprints near the left field wall. In front of us the Atlanta pitcher warmed up. Matt watched for a few minutes, then turned to me. "What are they waiting for?" he asked.

"Waiting?"

"How come they don't start?"

"Oh," I said. "The game starts at one-twenty. See the clock on the scoreboard there?"

"Bummer," he said.

I anticipated a show of glory. Here were two teams as mismatched as possible. Atlanta had played miserably all season, particularly lately, losing six games in a row.

I explained it to Matt, trying to help him understand the subtle significance of the day's game. To casual fans it existed as one game of many, one hundred and sixty-two total. But within my own belief system it became more than that. All that had happened previously combined now to form a preview of this game, just as this one must lend its traits to tomorrow's, increasing the appeal ever so little, day by day.

Matt listened, interrupting me only for a bag of peanuts. The organist sounded the cue, and we rose with the crowd for the national anthem. Matt stood straight as a scout leader. Finally the Atlanta batter stepped to the plate.

Part of baseball's appeal lies in its absolute unpredictability. Maddux walked the first three men. The fourth homered to center. Another walk and two errors followed. The Cubs were down by five runs before anyone was out.

Nothing dampens the day like falling behind in the first inning. The best chances to cheer never arrive, having been derailed in the wait for three outs. A murmur passed over us as the manager tramped to the mound, head down.

Matt sat in restrained silence, like everyone else. I looked at him, wondering what he thought. For some reason he sat with his thumb and forefinger pinching his nostrils closed. As I watched, his face turned deeper shades of red, and I was afraid he was having an asthma attack. "What's the matter?" I asked.

He jerked his head to the right. "*Cigar!*"

Two seats down the row a plump man in a Hawaiian shirt puffed on a Dutch Masters. Ball parks are one of the last bastions of the cigar smoker. In an odd manner the aroma, reminiscent of a certain era and style, smelled pleasant to me. I traded seats with Matt.

Atlanta's hitters cooled after their large lead, and the Cubs barely harmed the ball. So for a time almost no action occurred, at least of the kind most fans prefer.

Matt gazed at airliners gliding toward O'Hare, counted the number of beers lapped up by a fan in the first row, and stared at the scoreboard for minutes at a time, as if waiting for it to reveal a mystery.

From time to time I mentioned items I hoped might stir his interest: how I happened to see Shawon Dunston in a Burger King, where to buy a T-shirt, how to get to Harry Caray's restaurant. And I told him that I heard Greg Maddux drives a sports car.

"English or Italian?" he said. "Try and remember."

I didn't know.

He thought about it for a while. "Probably a Porsche," he said. Then he announced he was going to the restroom.

"You should wait," I said. "I always go when the other team is up to bat."

He smiled. "Dad, I have to go now."

While he was gone my attention drifted, so I was flabbergasted to find a baseball in my hands. I realized it was flying my way when my neighbors leaped to their feet. The ball bounced off a railing and onto some fingers that tipped it a couple times. Then it rolled down an arm and onto my stomach where I plucked it as easily as a bag of peanuts. I waved it high in victory, thinking Matt might appear any time.

Ten minutes passed before he returned. He missed not only my moment, but the other fans' also, as Andre Dawson, awarding us something in a drowned cause, hit a long, elegant home run, over the wall, above the bleachers and across the street.

"Know what happened?" I said.

"No, what?"

"Dawson hit one out."

"Oh, the home run," he said. "I saw it on the monitor."

I concealed the ball for an inning. My chance to show it came when an agile fan one box over grabbed a sharp foul just before it bounced back on the field.

"You mean you can keep the ball?" Matt asked, evidently having missed the dozen or so that had already been pocketed by fans.

"If you can catch it, yes—and by the way, here's one for you." I held the ball to him.

"Hey—all right," he said, reaching for it. "They sell them, huh?"

"No, this is a game ball, you can't buy a game ball."

"Yeah? Well, where did you get it?" He turned it over in his hands, reading the manufacturer's name to himself.

"I caught it. When you were gone."

"You caught it?" he said. "Gee." He put the ball down on the seat beside him, and for an inning or so his eyes tracked every foul that went into the stands, as if he were trying to reconstruct how I happened to catch one.

By now a share of the crowd had left, and the Cubs fell further behind.

"When are we going?" Matt asked.

I hate leaving early. The last time I did, the Cubs scored six runs in the ninth and won. The knowledge of what I missed still haunts me. It was as if I'd skipped the March on Washington because I was touring the Smithsonian. I reasoned it out to Matt.

"You mean you think they could still win?"

The score was nine to one. "You never know," I said.

Matt sat with a depleted stare until a pinch-hitter struck out to end the game. As we started down the ramp I glanced back to our seats, nearly buried beneath bags and empty wrappers. I nudged Matt's shoulder. "You forgot something."

"I did?" he said, slapping his pockets.

"That's all right," I said, stepping over the trash to retrieve it for him. "It's just a ball."

We heaved ourselves into the VW and cranked down the windows, anxious to feelh the breeze of movement. I turned the key but nothing happened. The battery cable had loosened again. I got pliers from the storage compartment, jiggled the cable several times, and tried again. No response.

I grumbled and sweat while Matt sat as expressionless as a ticket taker. I twisted and jerked the battery until the car shook. Only after I took the cable off and put it back on did it make contact, and the engine sparked to life. By then greasy dirt covered my face and hands. When I stepped out of the car to put the tools back the engine coughed and fluttered. Again Matt reached the accelerator in time to revive it. Finally we were moving, and I reached for a cigarette.

"Oh, oh, Dad. Remember my asthma." I flung the cigarette out the window.

As we rode Matt again scrutinized the roadways. "Well, what did you think of the game?" I asked.

"Neat," he said. He craned his head around at an auto sales lot, its presence marked by strings of fluttering pennants. "What did you think?"

Baseball had become associated with solitude for me. I moved from place to place in the stands. At home I watched televised games alone, with sharpened pencils, a pack of cigarettes and a quart of Coke. I seldom had a chance to talk the game and it became stored up in me like a child's secrets.

Using that day's contest as an example, I tried to relate to Matt my sense of the beauty and grace of baseball, and how important it is to recognize the irrelevance of who won or lost.

I hoped he grasped it. It seemed important that he understand my attraction to the game. "Do you agree with that?" I asked.

"With what?"

"That it doesn't matter who wins and what the score is."

"Oh yeah," he said. Then he yawned and put a foot up against the glove compartment. "But you know, it's like Bruce says—winners are winners and losers are nothing."

The air conditioner had quit and the room was hot as an attic. The woman in the office told me that the sign advising guests to turn the air off when leaving should not have been ignored. The machines overloaded causing the circuits to blow out.

The maintenance man had gone home for the day. I asked for another room. All were occupied. I suggested the woman call the maintenance man at home. She couldn't do that. I leaned on the counter. "I'll call him myself," I said. "What's his number?"

A plastic sign with smiling flowers hung from a string behind the cash register. It thanked me for not smoking.

"We don't have it," she said, folding her arms.

"You know something, lady — " A rattle of coins and a clunk interrupted me. It was Matt. As he pulled the top from his can of Pepsi he offered the woman a little smile. She smiled back. He walked out.

I grabbed a newspaper from a stack on the floor, paid for it and went back to the room. Matt lay on one of the beds, staring at the television, his head propped up by his forearm.

My plans had included a nice dinner after the game. We would go some place where we'd be served hearty food — a place where we could sit and talk, boy-to-boy and man-to-man.

But the struggles drained my enthusiasm for conversation. Matt seemed equally listless. He lay there staring at his program with the insipid look of a television watcher. By the time I got through the box scores in my paper it was dark. Matt left the TV long enough to bring food from the Dairy Queen next door.

We ate our burgers and fries in silence. My reflections of the game reminded me of the ball I'd caught. I'd had no time to examine it closely. "Can I look at your ball?" I asked.

Matt glanced around his bed. "Oh, I left it in the car. Want me to go get it?"

"Never mind," I said.

I tried to involve myself in his TV program. A man was plotting to sell one of his daughters into prostitution so that the other could take equestrian lessons and make it to the Olympics.

My dejection led me into thoughts of how unfair everything is. My time with my son was already effectively over. He'd watch TV into the night and sleep late in the morning, waking up with only time enough to prepare for his noon flight out.

He was engrossed in the movie. The would-be prostitute displayed remarkable wits in preserving her virtue, but the other daughter was being seduced by her riding instructor. The father decided to stick up a drug store.

For the first time in a year I wanted a drink, but I was too tired to move. I fell asleep thinking of baseballs and cocktail waitresses.

I woke up early and glanced out the window. I pulled on my pants and stepped outside. The day was bright and blue.

Traffic was light on Dempster. I lit a cigarette and started walking. A Tribune delivery truck rolled by, moving so slowly I could hear the driver whistling. The truck stopped and a fat bundle of papers landed on the sidewalk. CUBS BURIED BY BRAVES, the headline read, FACE METS SHOWDOWN TOMORROW. I turned back toward the motel office.

I had coffee from the vending machine. A man was on duty now. "Nice day out," he said.

I asked him for change for the pay phone. First I called United Airlines. Then I called the Cubs ticket office. I bought a newspaper. "Thank you," I said to the desk clerk. "Thank you."

Matt woke up while I read the paper. I watched him trying to stir himself, avoiding my look, not wanting conversation in the morning. Cranky, like me.

"How soon do we go the airport?" he asked when he came out of the bathroom.

"We don't," I said. "You're not going back today."

"But Mom told me— "

"It's all right, I called the airline. There's a flight tomorrow afternoon. Your ticket's already changed."

He stood before me, blinking. "What about Mom?"

"Don't worry about it. You can call her right now, if you want. Here's some change." I gave him a handful of quarters. "Tell her it gets in at seven-twenty tomorrow night."

Matt frowned, but he took the coins. "It's okay," I said. "Tell her it's for sure. You'll be on it—and guess what else," I said. "I got tickets for the game tomorrow."

He started for the door. "Tell her it's for sure," I said, but he was already gone.

I was pleased. We'd have to go to my apartment, but that was good— maybe its closeness was what we needed, along with more time.

Matt came back, looking unhappy. Maybe I should have handled the call myself, I thought, but I had no more wish to speak to her than I had four years earlier. "So what did she say?"

"Huh? Oh, nothing, nobody home."

"Well," I said. "Hang on to the coins. Just so we let her know before she leaves for the airport."

Matt clicked the TV on, then threw himself on his bed. I went in to shower. When I came out he was still there. I sat down.

"Listen, Pal. You do want to stay another day, don't you? Let me know if you'd rather go back."

He stared at the TV screen. "No, I want to stay," he said.

"I thought you'd like a chance to catch the game tomorrow, seeing as how the one yesterday didn't turn out so good."

"Right," he said.

"I just don't want to make you do something you don't want to."

"You're not," he said.

We had the full day before us. It seemed fair to let Matt decide what we'd do. He thought for a while. "As long as it's not for, you know, sex and stuff, do you care if a movie is rated 'R?'" he asked.

I looked up movie times, wondering if I should overrule him. It seemed a waste of a day, sitting in the dark.

The line outside the theater stretched into the parking lot, but Matt insisted the movie would be worth it. We shuffled along, listening to the talk of strangers. When we got near enough to see the ticket booth I remembered something.

"You got through to your mother, right?" Matt looked startled.

"I forgot," he said.

I checked my watch. He could still catch her, but barely. "Get going," I said, giving him a shove. "Call your neighbor if she's not there."

That was all I needed. His mother coming after me with the sheriff. "Tell them to explain everything," I said. "I'll watch for you inside."

I waited impatiently. I hate being late for a movie. Finally Matt came in sight, puffing and hugging a tub of popcorn. The usher rushed us in as the credits rolled, but nowhere were there two seats together. I took a place on the far side next to a guy in a White Sox cap while Matt found a seat down front.

Before the movie was five minutes old I wished I was still standing in line. It centered on two friends who went to Canada to avoid the draft. But soon they regretted it so they found their way to Asia where they killed every one they saw by kneeing them in the stomach or elbowing them in the throat. I went for a cigarette every twenty-five minutes, much to the annoyance of the Sox fan.

"How did you like it when they killed those VC in the helicopter?" Matt asked. We were sitting in Arby's near Water Tower Place.

"It wasn't my favorite part," I said. I looked out at the people along Chicago Avenue. Two blacks in berets were sharing a laugh over something in a newspaper. One slapped the other on the palm of the hand. They laughed some more. Having a good time. Shucking and jiving on the avenue.

"Of course you know that really wasn't what it was like in Vietnam." Matt twirled a straw in a glob of ketchup. "Were you there?"

I realized then that he knew nothing about me. I should have let it go, but I looked at him and saw his mother in his eyes.

"I know what a waste it was," I said. "All the friends I lost, all the hate that came of it . . . what do you think of all that?"

He thought it over. "Bruce says we could have won that war if we'd hit them early."

When we got to the apartment someone was in my parking place. It always angered me because I hated leaving the VW on the street in that neighborhood. As I pulled in to turn around a police car appeared in front of the next apartment. Then I noticed two people, a man and a woman, in the first car. As soon as she leaned to open the door I recognized her. Matt's mother.

Matt looked at me, wide eyed.

"You didn't get through," I said, as calmly as I could.

His mother walked toward us. "Matt, get in the car with Bruce," she said.

"Wait a minute," I opened my door. Then, at the same time, both the cop and Bruce opened their doors. Only Matt sat still.

"Matt, I told you to go with Bruce," she said.

I looked at Bruce. He was soft in the middle, but he looked like he'd played a little ball in school. Football, of course.

"I warned you," she said. A hint of her father's jowls emerged in her face. She shook her head as if she were speaking to Matt—or to me, long ago. She pointed her finger at me, and I felt the blood rising in my ears.

"Sir, we don't want any trouble." It was the cop.

I felt like laughing in his face. They always say that, but what they mean is don't make any trouble. Of course, it's all right for us to inflict it on you.

Matt got out of the car. He was crying. He walked toward Bruce. I couldn't look at the cop, and wouldn't face Matt's mother. So I stared at Bruce, wondering.

I was going to look weak in my son's eyes. There was no other prospect for me. In short, I thought, why not make a fuss. At worst I'd spend a night in jail. Charges would be dropped. It wasn't like I hadn't been through it before. I'd shove Matt's mother out of the way, then charge Bruce. The cop would have to grab me from behind. If he were slow I'd have Bruce on the pavement.

I'd left the VW running. The engine started sputtering. All of us turned in its direction. It caught and sputtered, caught and sputtered. Then it gave a wheeze and quit. We kept staring at it, as if waiting for it to do something more.

"Dad?"

Our attention shifted to Matt. He'd stopped crying. "It's okay," he said. "It doesn't matter anymore."

His mother looked at him, then at me. I felt something drain. Perhaps it was my will. Matt wiped his eyes with the bottom of his T-shirt. Bruce looked at his watch. The cop pretended to study the Cubs bumper sticker on the VW.

"Please, could we talk?" I said. These were the first reasonable words I'd spoken to her in three and a half years.

Matt's mother visited her sister while he stayed overnight with me. We had to report to her in the morning and again after the game. If we didn't show up at the airport by 5:30 a warrant would be ready.

Bruce left for the airport as soon as he could. They'd dropped everything when Matt didn't show up.

It was late when we settled in. Matt sprawled across the couch and flipped the TV on as if nothing extraordinary had happened in days. The sportscast reminded me once again of the baseball I'd caught. It was only the day before, but it seemed like seasons ago. I went out to the car and opened the door. There the ball sat, resting on the seat like a leftover apple on the day after a picnic.

The air was cooler now, cooler than the apartment, and the night felt pleasant. The sky shined with a yellowish twinkle through the clearness of the twilight. It signaled the approach of cold northern air.

I looked upward toward Orion, the Big Dipper, and others. Sighting Cassiopeia reminded me of how my own father had worked to point it out to me on a summer night far in the past. I'd found it impossible to see how that particular arrangement of stars formed anything. The more I looked, the less I saw. But when my resistance dissolved I saw it clearly, like a fine drawing, and as distinct as it must have been to ancient shepherds.

I've recognized Cassiopeia easily ever since. Now for the first time in a long time, I missed my father. I knew he'd be happy to know Cassiopeia stands as clear to me as it does to him, and it shines on both of us, just as it does on Matt.

He was asleep when I came back in. I watched him for a few minutes, then turned the lights out. During the night I awoke to find him standing by my bed, staring at me. But in the morning he said he slept all night, so maybe I dreamed it.

The cooling continued after dawn. The Chicago weather which can drag the temperature down forty degrees in a day did just that. The sky became gray and by lunch time the wind came up. Matt feigned enthusiasm about the game. We went only because of my hope that the romance of the ballpark would work its magic and fix everything that had gone wrong.

The Cubs carried over their previous ineptness. The wind off Lake Michigan decimated the happy bleacher crowd, leaving the rest, like us, huddled over hot cocoa, searching the gray sky for warmth. Before long it became too much, even for me. A newspaper rattled across our path and the wind whistled in the old iron beams as we hurried out, eager for the shelter of the car.

His mother stayed politely in the background at the airport while Matt and I shared tacos. I watched the clock, dreading what it would mean when our time together was over.

I knew there was a meaning, but it was out of reach. It existed in the way I linked my vitality to baseball. The potential required a backward study. In baseball what has gone is as important as the present. For me, a team or a game or a season has no definition until its moment has passed. And so it must be with Matt. To draw a conclusion while waiting with him at the airport was futile, no matter how much I was haunted by all we left unsaid.

But now it was too late. They called his flight. For the first time in four years we hugged. As he walked away, following his mother, he turned to hide a tear in his eye. I blinked hard.

"See you, Pal," I called out.

"See you, Dad," he answered. Then he was gone.

I watched the plane as it sat on the tarmac. I waved back at the waving hands visible in the airplane windows. The door shut with a clunk, the ramp drew back, the engine whine grew louder, and the plane rolled away. I stood for another ten minutes and watched as it left the runway, climbed hard into the dark sky, and turned to the east.

I walked to the car slowly. We'd shared less than three days, and yet I'd become used to his presence, and I missed him. I missed him walking behind me, searching for his fancy cars, calling me "Dad."

I climbed into the car and sat for a moment, wishing he were there in the other seat. Then something on the floor caught my eye. I picked up an old scorecard. Underneath it rested the baseball. I rubbed it up a little and tossed it in the air a couple times as best I could in the closeness of the car. Its heft and perfect roundness felt good. I thought of it flying around the horn, propelled by the trustworthy arms of the Cub infielders. I rubbed it again, placed it gently on Matt's seat, and pointed the car toward home.

The Habit of Despair

THE MPs were clean and quick, and the fine southern accents they carried for the fragments of communication required in the course of their work must have added a sting to Vernal's outlook. But they had their papers right. They came through the green and white storm door of the double-wide with its plywood add-on, and there in front of those pee-smelling and puffy-faced kids, announced that he, Private Vernal Gene Frew, also known as Vernal Eugene Olson, was under arrest for desertion from the United States Army.

Vernal lay flat on the couch by the wall where he'd tacked his seal skin, and across the room from the new TV he'd bought with the bonus money I gave him. He was strained from finger-wording his way through the coho story in *Field and Stream*, but to accommodate the MPs he raised his arms while they put cuffs on his wrists, and lifted his feet while they slipped irons around his ankles. Then they stood him up, and, one on each side, walked him out to the car commandeered from the island police department just for the occasion.

I knew Vernal well enough. I gave him a job after my friend Sid gave me a job running the hardware. I guess since Sid was acquainted with me from the old days he expected that I'd be drunk half the time and less able to think up ways to steal from him like his other managers had. He was partly right.

Sid insisted his life was headed for grander purposes than stove bolts and hollow point shells, and he wanted time to concentrate on finding

those purposes. The store was the only hardware on the island. The first
thing I did was figure out what items we sold that we had monopolies
on, then I had the clerks mark them all up twenty percent. Sid thought
I was a genius.

I'd been there maybe four weeks and was still swollen with authority
and good feelings when I met Vernal Frew. I was in the back when he
came in. I watched him as he approached, walking straight-spined the way
a shorter person will, but halting and careful, like he expected someone
might leap out from the Thermos display and give him a good scare.

"Y'all har-rin?" he asked.

Vernal had a bad eye—it wandered, curious and solitary—making it harder
to pay attention enough to understand him. "What's that?" I said.

"Help," he said. "Y'all need help? Um lookin' for work."

By then the commotion of his wife and kids caught up to him. There
were four children, all with black mop-head hair, though only one or two
were Vernal's. The baby, lighter-skinned than the others, was in its mother's
arms. Vernal introduced them all, including the baby, playing a finger under
its fat chin. But I only caught his wife's name, Wanda. She was an Eskimo
from St. Lawrence Island, and had the straight black hair and perfect skin
common to Indians and Eskimos. She lowered her chin and smiled toward
the floor when Vernal pronounced her name.

As it turned out my sporting goods man had just given his notice. I
asked Vernal if he knew anything about guns.

"Bin farn 'em all my life," he said.

I took a hunch, figuring he was pressed hard for a job, and I hired him cheap.
It was a good choice. Vernal moved a lot of merchandise for us. Eskimos
in from the villages liked him, and trusted him. They called him Bernal.

"Where's Bernal?" they'd ask, leaning over the handgun case, palms flat
on the glass. Vernal would hear them and come out of the back room,
happy to get away from the puzzle of invoices and stock cards.

"If it ain't Joe Tommy," he'd say. "Didn't know y'all was in town. Did
you get you a moose? I heard tell the salmon are runnin' in Shishmaref."

They knew Vernal had married an Eskimo, and even if she wasn't highly
thought of, they realized that marriage and his lack of book learning would
hold him to the country. They liked that he said he was from Tea Hook,

West Virginia, because it sounded so far away and because the place seemed like it might have something to do with the Civil War. He'd also gathered some local fame from a time he'd been a hero when his seal hunting party became stranded. But mostly they liked the benefit of his expertise with guns and the easy way he handled them.

"Now that would make you a quality piece," Vernal would say if he noticed a customer eyeing a particular hunting rifle, such as an average-priced Mossberg. "But first let me show you this here one, just in case you had in mind to go after seal." Then he'd reach for a Wetherby or even a Sako, knowing full well that seal was exactly what the customer had in mind.

Vernal would never hand the gun over directly. Instead he'd hold it just out of reach, delicately, sighting down the barrel, polishing the stock with his handkerchief, all the time talking up the virtues of that rifle – its accuracy, its range, its power. Only when his customer was primed would Vernal place the gun in the person's hands, holding it so it had to be received just above the trigger guard where the balance felt best.

Things worked. Sales went up, Sid stayed away. I felt enough in control that I started spending late afternoons at the Board of Trade bar. I noticed Wanda come in now and then with two or three girlfriends. They'd take a table near the juke box and listen to Ferlin Husky tunes. They talked a little, danced gently, smoked Kool cigarettes from one another's packs, and in an hour sipped maybe a third of a beer each. It was all harmless. They dropped their kids off at one of their many relatives just to be with other adults in an adult world for a while. It was less than the equivalent of a tea party in other places.

I might smile and wave to Wanda, keeping it proper and polite. She was Eskimo, I was white, and her husband was hired help. But one afternoon I was a little juiced, and though I knew it was off base, I asked her to dance. She looked at me like I'd called her a name.

"Me? I can't," she said. And she stared at the floor while I stood there with one arm stuck out, feeling foolish.

I should have let it go then, but there's always that mystery between men and women. It doesn't have to do with race or age or married, or rich or poor. They don't have to speak the same language. It doesn't even have to do with lust. There is a curiosity involved, and it includes both people, and the tiniest thing—just a glance is all—gets it going. And like many a habit, once the thing starts, it carries itself.

Not that there was any denying my interest. I caught the air of something in Wanda—a pleasurable spirit and smoky attractiveness. Her friends had the appearance of Eskimos, short and middle-thickened, like they were getting ready for winter. But Wanda was pinch-waisted and light. In her blue jeans she looked fit and ready, like a Montana cowgirl at a rodeo. And she had a way of tossing that tress of dark hair back over her shoulder as if it were a handful of troubles.

My luck started slipping when Sid got into one of his spells of interest in the store and found my microwave order—a mistake, I admit, since most of the outlying villages didn't yet have electricity. A couple days later the mail included a memo Sid sent from home, advising that purchase orders for high ticket appliances must hereafter be authorized by him. He signed his full name to the memo, middle initial included.

Vernal lived with Wanda and all those kids in a double-wide back of the gravel pit. I could see the place from the airport road. A propane tank leaned against the far end, its copper line coiling in through the corner of a window. Strips of loose plastic flapped in the wind against the plywood add-on. Vernal was drawing a hundred and forty a week before deductions. They were probably getting food stamps, and with Wanda being Eskimo they likely qualified for a little aid of this and that kind. Getting by, if you can call it that.

I let Gertie in the office know to bump Vernal up ten bucks a week, and when Sid learned of that I got another memo in the mail. When it came I made a draw slip for a hundred dollars which I covered by under-ringing the Evinrud that Jack Kanalak paid me cash for. I tucked the hundred in Vernal's shirt pocket behind his pack of Lucky Strikes. Tears came to the man's eyes. He took my hand in both of his. "I'm mighty grateful," he said.

By then I knew that I wasn't about to be retired from Sid's hardware with a pension and a party, so I figured I better help myself to some moving money. The department with the highest volume was sporting goods, and the department head with the least amount of business sense was Vernal.

A good combination. I started to skim from his register, ten or twenty at a time, just to see what would happen. I figured to up it to a hundred a day come hunting season.

After a few days—time enough for word of my generosity to pass from Vernal to his wife—I spotted Wanda at the Board of Trade and sent a round of Old Style to her table. I waited a few minutes before I walked over.

"Wanda, that's a pretty sweater you got on," I said. "New, ain't it?" I reached for her elbow. "Feel a little more like dancing today?"

I've never liked dancing. But when I pulled Wanda against my chest and tucked her arm under my own to begin the slow two-step, which was all I knew, I felt some of what people must dance for. I shuffled to the left, one step, then another, then a step back. Wanda followed. This was a woman who'd given birth four times in not many more years, but she was as light as a broom. She danced with me, stepping with me, giving me my way across and back the little wooden dance floor, while through the window the thin northern sun trickled in to mix with the stink of the beer and the smoke.

I found myself wondering about those four kids and their fathers, how many fathers were involved, and how many times it took to conceive the babies, and if they'd been goals of lovemaking or just some kind of accident. Wanda didn't talk. She would never let me know what she was thinking— love or hate. That was her way of defending herself, but I was working against it, drawing that resistance out of her and plugging it with curiosity. The song ended and Wanda stopped moving. I held on to her.

"Can I come see you sometime?" I said. She looked at the floor. I think she saw me in a new arrangement, like the way you might look at a relative that's just come into money—or maybe it was that big TV that I knew Vernal had put the hundred bucks down on.

"When?"

"Oh, on a nice afternoon, maybe when the kids are down for their naps. And when everything's good and slow."

She moved her foot back and forth on the floor as if to grind out a cigarette. Then she gave the toe of my boot a little tap, then another. "Vernal, he likes you," she said.

"Vernal's a good man."

"He's glad you hired him on. Working at the hardware."

"Can I come see you tomorrow then?"

"No, not tomorrow," she said, and she walked away.

I waited several days. The barge shipment came in on a Thursday. I marked the invoices with my grease pencil and set Vernal and the high school kids to shelving and pricing it all. Then I washed my hands real good and picked up a couple packs of Kools.

I left the Blazer parked out on the road, though anyone that came along could spot it and make the connection if they had the bent to look for those things. The four-year-old, sleepy looking in a raggedy Seattle Mariners T-shirt, answered my knock. I smiled. Wanda appeared behind him.

"Charlie, get back to bed," she said. I stepped inside. As Wanda herded Charlie to the back room I took my coat off. The TV already had a purple gob of jam or jelly smeared along one corner of the screen. The arm to a doll and a couple of fishing magazines were on the floor. Tacked to the wall over the couch was what I figured to be a trophy-size seal skin, all stiff-haired and mottled.

Wanda came down the hall, tossing her hair over her shoulder. She stopped at the corner where the hallway turns to the kitchen, listening for the kids' voices and the thumps they made jumping from the bed to the floor. Finally there was silence.

When I kissed her, her mouth was wide and ready. I put a hand on her breast and worked it until my fingers felt the nipple respond through the fabric of her blouse. I undressed her from the top down. In the manner of a first-time lover she seemed not to know if I wanted her to help. I twisted her bra off and she was naked and beautiful. I pulled her to the floor, not wanting to move from that corner and put the good mood at risk. Only when I was in her, braced for leverage against Vernal's new jam-stained TV, did Wanda break out of her shyness enough to make a sound.

The next time I came by we made love in front of the baby. The kid giggled and cooed, and so did the mother. All of it served to excite me and by the time we finished we'd writhed and slithered from one corner of that dirty rug to the other. After we lit up our Kools I asked Wanda about the seal skin.

Vernal had shot it, she said. He was real proud because he got it at the end of a hunting trip he'd taken with Wanda's two brothers and her father. They were in the long boat, had engine trouble, and drifted away from shore. They made a landing after two days, but it was foggy and they dared not move. They ran out of food the second day ashore, and were down to four rounds of ammunition. The three Eskimos had a conference and decided that Vernal should be the one to take the gun with the four bullets and look for game. It was an honor on top of the great responsibility, and it was with one of those bullets that he got the seal.

We'd been lying on the floor, and I heard a stirring from the back bedroom. One of the older kids was waking up.

"That's a thing to take pride in," I said. "Where'd he learn to shoot so good?"

"In the army, I guess." Wanda's hands were behind her back as she concentrated on fastening her bra.

"I didn't know he was in the army," I said. I'd been in the service myself, and I was sure I'd have noticed if Vernal had listed it on his application.

"Could be I'm wrong and it was somewhere else," Wanda said. "Men don't tell me all that's on their mind."

I pulled Vernal's application. There was a space with several lines for military service in which Vernal had written in little slanted letters a single word: none.

That afternoon I pinned Wanda between my hips and the kitchen floor of the double-wide, and she wrapped her dark legs around me while the baby spit and squawked in the high chair three feet away. Then she told me about Vernal. He'd even changed his last name. He hoped they'd never find him so far from West Virginia. It had been several years now, and he was just beginning to think that maybe they didn't care anymore, and that it might be forgotten after all. He'd never done much wrong except walk away. He even left his dress boots behind, in place beneath his cot and all spit-polished for inspection.

Wanda begged me not to let on to Vernal that I knew. "Don't worry," I said. "If you can't bank on me you're in real trouble." And I kissed her on the lips.

Three days later she told me not to come back for a while.

"You feel guilty?" I asked.

She laughed. "You whites, you're so stupid. This with you and me is nothing. The Eskimo way, the old ways, they got no—what do you call it—monogamy. That's your idea."

"Then why?"

"You can't see it." And she looked away, as always, avoiding my face. "I like dancing. You'll never take me where we could dance."

"Sure I will," I said.

Wanda put a fresh cigarette between her lips, and struck a match, but stared at its flame without lighting the cigarette. "I got four babies. By the time they're gone I'll be like my mother. Always cold. Coughing all the time in the night. The things I got right now is those kids, the new TV, and to dance with Vernal."

I stayed away a long time. Now, I watched her in the B.O.T bar and knowing she'd been available made it all the worse. It was unfair—I'd gone the hard miles of conquest, making pretending unnecessary. The only obligation we had left that was hooked to any truth was to please each other. I wanted her available again. I watched and listened while Ferlin Husky sang and Wanda danced.

Vernal asked to talk to me away from the store, and I spent an edgy two hours at the B.O.T. waiting for him. I decided if he confronted me I'd deny it, now that it was more or less over.

Vernal ordered a can of beer, any brand, no glass. I ordered an Old Style for myself and paid for both.

"It's about my gun sales," Vernal said, his bad eye scanning my face. "I figure somethin's off. Last weekend there wasn't but twenty-one hundred in the cash register. I sold more than that in deer rifles."

Deer rifles, I thought. I wanted to cry with joy. Still. "Are you sure?" I said.

"As I'm settin' here."

I listened, watching that nervous eye, trying to read everything. But the rest of his face showed nothing. Trying to find meaning in it was like plumbing the expressions of a goat. I thanked him for coming forward, and asked him to please not say much while I looked into the situation on my own.

The next day I made the call to Fort Richardson. They pushed me along a command chain of five different people, and I kept telling the same story. In between, they called me back twice, asking for more details. In a few days, a man in a suit came in the store, looked around, and was gone on the evening flight. He was there just long enough for me to know.

The Aleutian fog blew in the day they arrested Vernal. The plane couldn't get out directly so they took him to the city jail to wait.

I'd been a little out of sorts so I started drinking around eleven, nipping from a bottle I kept in my file drawer. By the middle of the afternoon I was bleary and mixed-up from what daylight and alcohol do to the system, and I got a notion that I wanted to see Vernal before they flew him away for good.

The MPs at first would hear none of it. But the store had helped out with the police department fund raising, and the chief told them I was all right. They said I could have five minutes, and I had to stand six feet away from the prisoner.

Vernal was in a cell alone, down the corridor from where they housed the drunks, the pot heads and the wife beaters. They let all of them have radios, and the radios blared with the same tunes you had to pay for in the Board of Trade. Vernal shook his head when he saw me, as if he'd just had a piece of bad luck.

I spoke first. "Vernal, I'm sorry about this. But don't worry, they'll soon get it cleared up in your favor." I knew there was zero chance of that, but I had to say something.

"No, no," he said. "Wasn't none of your doin'."

I'd sobered up a little, and was starting to feel uncomfortable. The other prisoners turned their radios down, and I felt like everyone was listening to me. I asked Vernal if he needed anything. He shook his head.

I told him the job would still be his when this was all over. He smiled at that and shook his head again, as if it was a shame I couldn't seem to understand the serious nature of what had happened. It was warm in there, and I started to sweat, and I was tired. Vernal stood there, a hand on each of two thick bars, staring at me with that one direct eye while the other looked up, down, here and there. I was unsatisfied with the visit, and with myself. I could think of no more to say, and I wanted nothing but to leave.

I reached to shake hands, but remembered the six foot rule, and changed the shake into a little wave.

"Eddie?" he said.

"Yeah Vernal?"

"I just wanted to let you know I liked working for y'all."

"Don't mention it," I said.

"I'll tell you, Eddie," he said. "I never had a job I liked 'til you gimme that one. I love to think of the way them old boys looked at me when I'd hand them a firearm, all bright and smelling of oil and gun bluing. They figured I really knew what I was talking about, didn't they Eddie?"

"And you did, too," I said.

"Eddie?"

"Yeah?"

Vernal licked his lips, searching for more words, more ways to express his laid-open feelings — but he'd exceeded his limits. "I'm just tickled to know ya'," he said.

The weather broke that evening and the plane took off. I drove over to the double-wide, and Wanda let me in. Vernal's magazine was still on the floor, open to a photo of an Oklahoma Chevy dealer straining to hold his salmon to the camera. It was probably the picture Vernal was looking at when the MPs crashed in. Now he was 27,000 feet in the air and on his way to fifteen years of hard labor.

The tension of everything brewed a sexual hunger in me that wasn't to be put off. I nudged Wanda toward the hallway, past those black-haired kids watching TV. But Wanda wouldn't be nudged. The more I pushed, the more she stood her ground.

"What's wrong?" I said. I knew it wasn't the kids, and I was pretty sure she wasn't all that choked up about Vernal.

"I was just thinking I'd like to dance," she said. "Dance me back to the bedroom."

The kids were watching a show with background rock music that jangled the whole place. I did my best, bumping my hip into Wanda's crotch, following the beat, sliding along the ridges of the paneling to the bedroom.

"Vernal, he could dance," Wanda said. "Even at the Legion Hall with that concrete floor—he made it feel like the carpet at the Captain Cook Hotel."

We made love on her bed, on Vernal's bed. Then I stood up to put my clothes on. Wanda just lay there, with her legs parted a little, stroking the top curve of one breast where she said it stung a little, from my teeth.

"You turned him in, didn't you?" she said.

I fiddled with my clothes, shaking them out. "What was that?"

"You told on Vernal." Her chin was angled down, like she was searching for something on her breast.

"Goddamn," I said. "How could you even think that—for one thing he was the best gun salesman I ever saw. And for another, I like him. A whole hell of a lot more than you do, probably."

I was pleased with the last thought, and I let it hang in the air so it would be there and ready to bump into her own arguments. She stopped rubbing her breast and looked at me.

"You know something, Eddie," she said. "You're an asshole and I wouldn't give you a bullet if I had a bucketful of them."

She lay there and I felt her dark eyes burn into my back as I pulled on my shirt and my pants, then my socks and boots. And while I dressed I thought about Vernal.

There was something in him that I'd been reaching to when I saw him in jail. It was in his face, and in his eyes. His expression had things to say, ideas too complicated for his words. His face offered a recognition, a granting that he did know who he was, and where he was going, even if it was nowhere. It was a taking up of the habit again, the habit of despair. It wasn't just acceptance, it was that he was glad to have that acceptance. He was already serving those fifteen years, and Wanda and the babies and his job and the TV were all just stops along the way. Vernal was a guy who had to grab his happiness fifteen minutes at a time, and even then he lived knowing that his pitiful bit of joy could be gone, just like that.

That's all he'd get in his life, but then I realized—why the hell should I care—it could have been me, and no one told either of us we deserved any better.

The kids were still watching their show when I came out of the bedroom. For a minute I stood there in front of Vernal's seal skin, watching the kids and the TV, but I was anxious to leave—I didn't care to be there when Wanda came out.

But before I left I went to the kitchen and found an old dishrag that I doused in warm water. I came back to the TV and worked on that purple jam stain until the screen looked as bright and clean as when Vernal first saw it. Then I tossed the rag back toward the kitchen sink, picked up Vernal's magazine from the floor, and closed the storm door behind me.

People Like You

AT FIFTY-FIVE Loestroem is on disability from Madison and in no particular hurry to see the summer end when he falls upon the reckless notion that it is time at last to visit Rosie—and perhaps to make amends. Why not? He owes her that at least.

Grand Forks looks better than he expected—the elms over the English Coulee, the cobblestone of Central Avenue, the architecture in bashful imitation of the colleges back east. He drives straight to the house from memory. Stiff from hours behind the wheel, he stands at the door, hears the chain rattle, the bolt slide. Loestroem is agitated. *Leave now*, he thinks. The door pops open with a shudder. A thin faced young man stares through the narrow slant of light. This would be Jeffie.

"She's dead."

Rosie is dead? When?

The day before Mother's Day, Jeffie tells him.

Loestroem is stunned. He wants to sit down, but Jeffie's not helpful. Young people. Could Jeffie remember him? He was four or five. In his twenties now, he ought not to look like he does, with rooster-comb hair and a nasty leer. The sun hits the mirror of the van. Rosie. Gone. "You know who I am then?"

Jeffie stares, holding the door open the width of his foot, the rank odor of cooking grease behind him. "You the guy from Wisconsin?" He pronounces it Wes-consin.

Loestroem nods and offers his hand. He feels better. "Andrew Loestroem."

"I know. She always said you'd show up." Jeffie takes the hand but lets go at once. The opening narrows. "She said she didn't want you notified. So you should leave."

Loestroem forces an embarrassed smile. "What?"

"Get away. I don't need *you* here."

Jeffie's lilting way of talking, squeezing the ends of his sentences through his nose frightens Loestroem. He's grateful when the young man says, "That's all I'm gonna tell you."

Loestroem glimpses a dark coffee table cluttered with small hand tools, a leafless potted plant, a scatter of magazines. Nothing familiar. The door closes. The bolt clicks into place.

He met Rosie over a bridge table, Loestroem taking the place that night of Lem—a photographer. A photographer who traipsed the valley with a pocket atomizer squirting prairie flowers to give the appearance of dew. Lem framed an assortment of those teary blossoms and mounted them on a pegboard that he hauled to Art-in-the-Park shows in his VW bus, but no one wanted them. They were too fine, too workmanlike. (*Reader's Digest* stuff, Rosie said.) Lem made his real money snapping the smooth faces of grade schoolers with wild hair and shirts buttoned to the chin.

Loestroem hadn't wanted to go—meeting new people intimidated him—but he could scarcely turn down the invitation, considering. And then—surprise! He enjoyed himself. His luck at cards and the free-flowing beer opened him up. There *was* warmth and good will in the frozen North, at least in the Tait household.

He dazzled them at bridge, bidding six diamonds twice in a row. While it was Rosie's husband Lawrence Tait whose classes he'd teach that semester, and who he was therefore trying to impress with his wit and attentiveness, it was Rosie herself whose face lit up when Loestroem spoke of McGovern's chances, the beauty of the Badlands, the need for teachers to get out in the field.

"My five years with those inner-city kids was the most honest teaching I'll ever do," he said, little realizing how prophetic that was.

"Larry, *you* should try that." Rosie's long fingers shuffled the cards.

"Perhaps when I return I will," said Tait. "I'm full of surprises, my dear."

Rosie snorted. "I suppose you'll manage to find partners in London."

Tait spoke into his cards. "It's Cambridge, as you very well know."

Tait's partner April, who in her late forties made a safe third to Loestroem's fourth, felt compelled to speak up. "What choice I suffer to test my love twixt the frolics and my master."

Rosie rolled her eyes. "God, April. Really."

"Who's that from?" said Loestroem.

"From April," said Rosie in a flat voice, taking the trick with the ten of clubs.

"I admit to envy," said April. "Five months immersed in Chaucer. Lawrence is fortunate."

Tait heaved a resigned sigh. "At my age I deserve fortunate."

April snorted in derision. "You're not as old as I."

"Nearly, my dear, a good deal closer than these other two, if the truth be known."

Rosie's husky voice spoke, "Down with truth." She made a show of gathering the cards. She loved the large gesture. "Who dealt that?"

Loestroem admired the cavalier way the Taits entertained. An aluminum pan of Rice Krispy bars beside a stack of paper napkins, a not-too-clean Mr. Coffee machine, an open bag of ripply potato chips. Several cans of beer, loosened from their plastic sleeve, warmed on the drainboard.

They switched partners. April raised herself with a strain. "Are you a family man, Mr. Loestroem?"

"One wife and two children. We decided it's best they stay in Chicago with her parents since the appointment seems to be temporary."

April peered over her cards. "You're welcome here. You're a fine bridge player."

Rosie said, "You'll barely get to know us in one semester."

Loestroem became expansive. "Unless the department insists on creating a chair for me." April cleared her throat gently. Tait who was due to rotate into department head upon his return gave off a light grunt, his folding chair creaking.

A thump and a wail sounded from the bedroom. Rosie spoke without looking up. "Larry, see what Jeffie wants."

The phone rang. Rosie reached a long arm for it, coiling the cord between her knees. "He can't talk now," she said.

"Who was that?" said Tait, returning and smelling of Listerine.

Rosie dropped the queen of hearts gently. "The same one. Is he a student or not?"

Tait turned his palms ceiling-ward in feigned innocence. "How would I know?"

"Please do something about him."

April looked over her glasses at Rosie. "Do you have the king too?"

Rosie shook her head sadly. "Nope."

"That means she does," April said to Loestroem.

April played her jack. Rosie took it with the king. April pulled at her fiery red hair in mock terror. "I haven't had a finesse work this month!"

With Larry fetching a beer and April in the bathroom Rosie and Loestroem found themselves elbow to elbow at the card table. The closeness was immense. Rosie fixed a loose stay in her hair. "Are you a skier?" she asked.

As was his habit, Loestroem analyzed the question. "Why do you ask?"

"You have a peculiar walk, like your feet are too heavy."

"It's not from skiing. I hate the cold."

"Well children," boomed Tait. "What *are* we talking about?"

At the Gateway Best Western Motel wheat fields touch the redwood fence. Beside the pool and veranda tourists rest, drinking cocktails in plastic glasses. In the parking lot Loestroem has noticed many cars with Manitoba license plates. It's four-lane now all the way to Winnipeg. They come down in droves, the Canadians, to take advantage of the favorable exchange rate. Happy Harry Markets (heart) Canadian shoppers! proclaims the billboard on I-29 near the University Avenue exchange.

But, according to CKY on Loestroem's car radio, and a well-written letter in the *Herald* from a clothier in Morden, the situation is ruinous for small businesses along the border. If the provincial government fails to act soon every town within an hour's motoring to the States is going to dry right up.

This bothers Loestroem. *Dry right up*, they said, and he sees caked-mud images of raggedy-hat farmers in the Depression. One more in the incessant line of injustices. Ever since they asked him to take early retirement—he could have fought it, pushed an appeal—he's become aware of all the great wrongs in the world. He can picture himself a crusader like Chavez or Nader. But already he's not sure which way to point the van next. He thinks of abandoning this poolside comfort and driving to Morden, searching out the dry goods merchant, and buying his most expensive sweater. He sighs. His thickened middle and withered legs becoming hairless near the ankles disgust him. The sun has moved and Loestroem must slide his aluminum chair to move with it. He strains, grunting, and spills his drink. So much fixing required. He finds himself teary-eyed again. A mother in an old-fashioned bathing cap is tugging on the hand of her daughter, pulling her from harm's way. He's lonely. Except for Jeffie he's not spoken to anyone whose name he knows in two weeks.

He watches a chubby boy belly-flop from the low board. Loestroem thinks that if the boy tucked his chin in, he might do better. The old instinct to instruct is nudging him—he always liked the one-to-one idea of teaching. He realizes he fooled everyone. Because he was educated, a professor, more was expected of him. In truth, he can't distinguish sine from cosine, has no idea how fuel injection works, and encounters ongoing difficulty with I, me, and myself. He knows literature and poetry, and the older he gets the less sure he's become that he knows much of them, the knowledge being non-cumulative, unlike driving a taxi or restoring Florentine art. He disappoints others when he points this out. His is the face of a man who lets people down.

In the room he dwells on these, his deficiencies. While glad to be free from the rages of youth, he's alarmed at his condition. He has a disorder, though he's not sick like Lem was. His is the rather tiresome, out-of-fashion malady having to do with the fruit of the barley. He expected when they pressured him out (fired him, he will say, to acquaintances though not to friends) that at last he would do something about his malady. He's surprised he hasn't, and knows he will in time. But poor Lem, blackmailed by the mother of a ten-year-old he seduced. Bled dry he goes to the cops and gets the maximum. Eighties hysteria. No one from the old bridge crowd of that spring has been untouched by adversity. Loestroem wonders what became of April. There's a phone book beneath the oversized room service menu, but her last name has escaped him—though he easily recalls the name of her black Lab. No matter. He'll sleep now and the name will return to him in the morning. It was Italian, he thinks.

※ ※ ※

Such a hit was Loestroem he was again invited for bridge, this time only days before Tait jetted eastward.

Loestroem began the evening verbose—the style he employed the first night. On the way over he'd heard Eric Sevareid's sonorous radio voice announce that J. Edgar Hoover had died. This failed to interest anyone—nor did his wordiness. These people were taut, on edge, concealing something. He shouldn't have come.

"You'll have to be Rosie's partner," Lawrence Tait said. "She hates the way I bid."

Rosie scowled at him. "That's not what I said."

Tait liked to hold his cards against his ample stomach, angling them for a glimpse. "You *know* you'll enjoy the games more when I'm gone."

"Who knows if we'll even play," said Rosie.

Like April, Rosie chain-smoked when she played cards. Everyone smoked and maintained good enough health—except Larry whose cherry complexion and bulging eyes revealed strain. "Rosie, you must cut down," said Larry.

April studied the dummy. "Hold the table talk," she said, laying a card down.

Loestroem, ill at ease, forgot what had been played.

"There!" said April. "Last three are mine. That's game and rubber."

"Sorry, I'm playing like a bonehead tonight," said Loestroem to Rosie.

"So you noticed," said Larry.

Rosie turned on him. "I hope you find your manners in England."

April drove home with Baron, her Labrador who always waited in the car. Tait excused himself after insisting Loestroem stay. He was gone for two, five, ten minutes.

"Goodness, what's your husband doing?" asked Loestroem.

Rosie snuffed her cigarette in the big green and white UND ashtray. "Watching the kids sleep." With her slender fingers she placed a Beatles record on the turntable. "He's convinced they won't care about him when he gets back."

Loestroem agonized over etiquette. Was it time to leave? Rosie offered no clue. The music eased his tension. "I had a dream about you," he said, smiling.

Rosie looked alarmed. "Oh, what?" She was a tall woman, fair-skinned

and fair-haired, with a graceful but unnatural posture, suggestive of a nagging parent.

"I'll tell you some time," said Loestroem, his face taking on a seriousness
befitting the rising stakes.

Rosie's pale cheeks flushed. "When?"

That moment Loestroem realized they might become lovers—and he
was pleased, even if it was more the *idea* of making love to another woman
that was important, not the actual carrying out. In those days the abstract
counted for more.

✳   ✳   ✳

On this breezeless evening, Loestroem retraces a walk he and Rosie took
through Lincoln Park twenty years ago. He crosses Belmont Road at 17th,
recalling a candy store with a purple door and a cracked plate-glass window displaying a poster of the Philip Morris bellhop. Rosie borrowed money
for Sugar Daddies, later counting out thirty-eight cents from Jeffie's Fighting
Sioux piggy bank in repayment.

A jogger clip-clops toward him, staring earnestly through those round
eyeglasses that are again in fashion. The park looks foreboding. The wooden
ski jump is gone as are the swings. A metal fence with discouraging twisted
wires lining the top marks the south boundary of the golf course. Loestroem
recrosses Belmont and turns west toward the old neighborhood, thinking.

She'd been through the Panama Canal, slept with a man from Kenya
who wore sandals made of acacia bark and whose skin, she said, was so
black it *glowed.* She'd given away a baby, saved her brother from drowning
in the backyard pool, and ridden in the Rose Bowl Parade where Danny
Kaye kissed her cheek. All before her twentieth birthday. She married
Larry and everything stopped. She never got out of Grand Forks and the
wooden-sided, one-story house with the cement-block foundation.

Loestroem views the place from 20th, not wanting to go closer, needing
no more of the joyless stick Jeffie with his hostile eyes. The house and
wrought-iron pillar supporting the porch roof is a mirror image of the
house across the street, and a flipped-over floor-plan of the dwelling on
each side. The houses are in rows, two rows back-to-back forming blocks,
the blocks forming neighborhoods.

Once it meant sanctuary.

He's returning to 15th where the van is parked when he remembers a graveyard on the hill overlooking the river. It was separated from the golf course by a stand of hackberry and black oak that for some reason became the frequent target of lightning. Two hours of daylight remain.

His aging body protests the climb. The newer section stands out and he finds the grave easily: Rose Willet, appropriately on a rose-colored stone. She returned to her maiden name. The stone is set into the ground flat the way they put them now to allow the mower to pass. The plot is re-sodded with squares of soil, the grass not yet grown together on the borders. This is an unshaded area. Pale-skinned Rosie must hate the summer.

Loestroem surveys Rosie's silent neighbors and sighs. All these graves, the stones in their unchanging plainness, designed to remind us of what—the permanence of death? We already know that. Or of everlasting life. But that's not apt—the stones weather, the polished marble wearing until the surface is pitted and blank. Meanwhile, seventy-two inches down metal corrodes and bones return their calcium to earth. All those simplifications. We want such easy answers.

He stares at the stone, reading it again, then realizes they have the birth date wrong. Or do they? He shakes his head at his own gullibility. She was three, actually four years older than she said. The lie hurts him. He's being punished anew. Even the dead hold grudges.

✳ ✳ ✳

They sat, the three of them, waiting for Rosie to return to the table from Jeffie's bedroom. Lem found a calender of Elizabethan proverbs Larry had sent. He read aloud, "April damp and warm does the farmer no harm."

"Oh, my!" said April, and the laughter reawakened Jeffie.

Lem, the least educated of the bridge group, was a fountain of information. He knew the complete lyrics to *Pirates of Penzance*, where in Grand Forks to buy the right kind of cheesecloth to make chokecherry syrup, what the dean of women said to the lieutenant governor. He also kept a collection of eight-millimeter stag movies.

Loestroem concluded that the bridge group liked Lem as an oddity, but preferred keeping him at a certain length, like a pet snake. His lore was broad, not deep. Strangely enough Lem wound up in Madison also, which was where he came to his own unhappy derangement.

Something about Lem aroused Loestroem's impulse to confide. "Rosie has modern ideas," he told him. "She lets the boy barge right into the bedroom."

According to Lem, Rosie had all the brains. "She has a great curiosity," he told Loestroem, speaking through clouds of Camel smoke, breezy and self-confident, in the manner gays assume when the subject is sex between straights—as if they're bemused and a little bored. "And a wonderful loyalty. But watch it—she fibs."

Rosie was a daughter of a Ph.D. who was the daughter of a Ph.D. All that paper. All those diplomas. That constant esoteric conversation was too much for her. She dropped out of Smith and toured Europe for a year, riding a Honda motorcycle with a basketball player from Schenectady. My *New York Yankee*, she called him, switching sports to suit her purpose.

They chose Denmark for the baby because the Danes maintained a liberal tolerance and a good command of English, and because they promised to place the child in the arms of loving parents. But the old woman with the Accutron on her thin wrist who worked over Rosie muttered in some unintelligible tongue that was neither Danish nor English, and held a cloth reeking of chloroform to Rosie's face.

"*Chloroform!*" said Rosie, to Loestroem when she told him the story, which was the first of more than a hundred times they made love during the four months. To Loestroem, the fantastic part of the story was that when Rosie came out of the Danish hospital her New York Yankee was gone, vanished on the Honda.

"What did you do," said Loestroem, sympathy rippling through his chest.

The sheet slid from one of Rosie's perfect knees. "What else? I wired Larry for money and flew home."

When they drank too much, as they did with regularity, Rosie liked to sing a ditty.

> *My girl's from Smith.*
> *She talks like thith,*
> *Except when we kith.*

"Andy's taking Larry's place," she said, introducing him to two of Tait's former students in Duffy's where they drank green beer on St. Patrick's day.

They shook his hand and filled his glass from their pitcher. And when they sang "Sweet Rosie O'Grady," Loestroem chimed in though he couldn't sing a lick. He knew they understood—those alert students with their long hair—but he was grateful nonetheless.

Against the backdrop of spring with its burgeoning hawthorn and thunderstorms lighting the sky horizon to horizon Loestroem became a Romantic poet, ennobled by affection. He read Coleridge aloud, skipped lunches to call Rosie, brought her the Cadbury's chocolate in red foil that she loved.

On Rosie's birthday they strolled through a stand of raggedy birch where Rosie made a nest of dry grass. Not far away golfers walked, paused for a shot, walked again, hurrying to beat the setting sun glinting orange on their spindly clubs.

"Look, there's a plant that's getting leaves. What kind is it?"

Loestroem had no idea. He gazed at the tiny bush, hoping something would come. "I should know."

"You're such a worry-burger," she said. "Make up a name like Larry would. Milky frogwort."

Loestroem liked that, that Larry could come up with quick answers. He thought of himself as lacking imagination.

As Rosie studied the trudging golfers, incongruously agitated for all their peaceful surroundings, her face suddenly brightened. "Want to try something crazy?" she said. "Look, they left the lock off." She pointed toward a flat-roofed shack back of the cart path.

They waited, timing their move. Over the rise a pudgy man swung, all arms, the ball shot toward the distant rough, a crack followed. Rosie went first while Loestroem pulled the door closed.

Light-headed with excitement, they spread a layer of clean white rags over the tool bench. Rosie tugged her sweatshirt up. "I feel like Lady Chatterly."

The romance at first escaped Loestroem. "What if they lock us in?"

"What if they do?"

They pretended to giggle at the chilly air on naked skin, but they weren't in a giggling situation. Laughter turned to moans.

Rosie said, "It's always sex, isn't it?" They made their way home, cutting past the horseshoe courts, relieved to be free of the insecticide-smelling air in the greenskeeper's shack.

"Not always. George Eliot and her man spent evenings reading from the Encyclopedia."

Rosie walked head down, as if taking no comfort from George Eliot. A loud clank startled them. Someone was playing horseshoes in the dark.

"I love you," Loestroem said, taking her arm.

"You'll regret that," she warned.

It was true—he did, but he needed to say it to dispel the other notion. *Besides,* he thought, we regret so many things. All the should-have-beens. One more remorse gets lost in an ocean of regret. If he hadn't broken his ankle in 1956, he'd never have learned to play bridge. If not for Robert Louis Stevenson, he'd never have become an English teacher, and if his mother had followed her four sisters into tiny white caskets during the 1918 flu epidemic he'd never have been born.

Rosie kissed him on the mouth. "Right now I love you too, Andy."

The phrase brought gladness to Loestroem—though he knew that like an elaborate joke, it was most effective with the first telling. More memorable to him was his realization that his life had taken an enormous shift, that all the old comforting faces and environments were about to change, that he would not be raising his own children.

＊ ＊ ＊

The big Panasonics in the Gateway are not secured to their holders as they tend to be in most motels. This troubles Loestroem. Temptations await everywhere. He sits up and rubs Solarcaine into his sunburned face. The TV offers a commercial with a black automobile salesman who is making huge self-conscious gestures, as if challenging you to prove you're not a bigot by purchasing a car from him. Loestroem takes the ice bucket and room key, shuffling along in the uncomfortable brown sandals that have tortured his toes for a quarter century.

An elderly man in striped bib overalls is bending down, pulling weeds from the cracks in the sidewalk. This also bothers Loestroem. He likes the look of the greenery, the idea that vegetation flourishes in unlikely places. They can't leave well enough alone.

Loestroem recalls how, with the master of the house absent, the Tait backyard revealed its winter accumulation of trash and paper as the snow melted. Two decades later he can still picture the clutter as it appeared through Rosie's bedroom window. He has only a vague recollection of the walls in his own apartment (cement block coated with a rubbery lime-colored paint), yet every detail of Rosie's house stands out as if he'd grown up in it. The kitchen window crank that turned the wrong way, the orange stain in the bathtub, the rich cedar smell of her bedroom closet.

He is weeping again.

✳ ✳ ✳

Friday nights Rosie prepared deep-dish pizza, April brought wine, Lem entertained the kids with a magic show. This was how educated people lived. Company, music, conversation. You could talk about Keats un-self-consciously, make jokes about Agnew. You could take a drink any hour of the day. How unlike his own Illinois childhood where he hid pictures from *Esquire* in a syrup tin with a carrying handle. How different from the home of his in-laws where colored sheets seemed a frivolous, Hollywood affectation, where laughter and energetic debate were regarded with suspicion.

He actually *enjoyed* the ongoing feuds and departmental campaigns. Tenure, publication, broaden the curriculum. So many hours of talking, so many fine points in need of discussion. Such was the way of higher learning, and Loestroem understood it. That spring he decided the academic world was the world for him. He'd spend the next twenty years, students and their ideas blowing past him like sleet, searching out the joy he knew so briefly.

Rosie liked beer but complained of the calories. Loestroem thought *she* looked thin as a wand, but he was gaining weight. He switched to vodka, sweetening it with fruit juices, but never lost the weight — carting it around year after year, one more reminder of his self-indulgence that long-ago spring.

Loestroem would recall piles of child clutter — clothing in washed-out solid colors, one-eyed bears crusty with dried milk. He was aware of the kids as a potential for attention — asleep one wall removed — rather than a fact of interference. When he thought of them years later they became invisible. Only Meghan warmed to him, regarding him perhaps as sent by God to keep Mommy from loneliness. She flew to him while mopey Jeffie watched. When he held her, red-mouthed with her soapy girlish smell, she felt weightless beneath his guilt.

Rosie offered no guidance, made no effort to resolve Loestroem's ex-cruciating paradox. He was free to like or ignore the children as he pleas-ed. One night Meghan called him *Daddy*.

"What's the difference?" insisted Rosie. "As long as people know they're loved."

"How about Larry?"

"I don't *not* love him," she said. She was pulling her sweatshirt over her head, a gesture that pleased Loestroem. "But I know one thing. I'll never go without a sex life again."

That surprised Loestroem. "How did three kids get started?"

"Business is business and pleasure is pleasure," she answered, her voice untroubled.

Loestroem's necessary life, his remote and nagging *other* existence, began filling with a long-distance, convoluted story suggested by Rosie. To the wife in Chicago he said he had a friend, Frank, who lived alone and had no phone. That's where he spent evenings—playing bridge and yes, Frank smoked marijuana.

"Mari*jua*na? Andrew Edgar Loestroem? Excuse me, but that doesn't sound like you," said Jo, her telephone voice pushing into place each separate syllable. "Is *that* what they do up there? Aren't you a little *old* for that kind of behavior?"

When he felt threatened Loestroem became pedantic. He wanted to point out to Jo that her objections made *her* sound old. But he hated con-frontation. Arguments depressed him. Anyway, he wanted a quick end to the conversation. Rosie was waiting in her car with the kids. They were driving to the base for the air show. The prospect of watching the Blue Angels soaring above the cares of the people below cheered him. "How's your money holding out?" he said.

"Well. Finally you ask. Thanks to Daddy we got the ten-speed fixed. I wrote about Music Camp. There's a fat envelope here from Southern Illinois, English Department it says. And Andy, honestly, that jumper you sent for Lizzie's birthday? She'll grow out of it by fall."

To Loestroem, Tait's return and the coming of summer meant the death of joy. The weekly letter from Larry to *his* family brought it closer. Rosie handed the letters over, insisting Loestroem read them. He was having a grand time, said Tait. A term abroad was very much what his constitution required. And his colleagues were so brainy. He raved about his graduate assistant who was simply *marvelous*. Marvelous was one of several words Tait had picked up. Middleton Smythe (pronounced with a long Y, said Tait, ever the teacher) was the name of this assistant. Middleton, the second of three sons of a Welsh sheep herder, took much ribbing over his name and what precise planners his parents must have been. But enough of all that. Would Rosie be a dear and mail more of his hypertension pills? The chemists in the countryside were impossible. Oh yes, he'd run to the continent a fortnight ago with Middleton where they'd caught the galleries.

Loestroem set the letter on the counter. "Run to the continent. Which one, I wonder, he doesn't seem to say."

"You see how he keeps asking about our bridge nights?"

"No, I didn't get that far."

"He wants to know if we've become close friends."

"What'll you tell him?"

"The truth. I don't lie to Larry."

No more did Loestroem make a pretense of parking down by the Catholic church, or of returning to his apartment on Dartmouth for the night. His apartment spooked Rosie—the single bed with its striped mattress, the cold checkerboard tile floor, the little triple-frame photos of Jo, tiny in her blue cashmere, and the kids, their unaccusing eyes scarcely guessing upon whom they gazed.

When he agreed to take the temporary position on the frozen plains Loestroem envisioned immersing himself in his dissertation. Texts lay about, face down with spines bent. He lowered his Remington from the chair to the floor so Rosie could sit. "I *have* to get to work on this," he said.

Rosie sighed. "Mother dragged home scads of her students' dissertations. Boxes full. She'd pile them in the corner like bricks to make her clay pots reach the window."

Loestroem had just been granted a three-year extension. "All that research used for bricks?"

"What's the point? No one's interested."

"Let's hope the committee at Champaign won't feel that way."

Rosie surveyed the piles of books with their satiny Chester Fritz Library labels. "Don't worry. You'll never finish it."

She was there to help him pack a suitcase to return to Chicago for spring break. Underwear, white shirts with button-down collars, casual slacks for outdoors. "I better take ties," he said. "For church."

Rosie had a habit of biting her upper lip when confronting a difficult question. "Are you coming back?"

Loestroem closed the suitcase, snapping the catches into place. In fact the possibility of staying in Illinois had been expanding like a thunder cloud, promising his salvation. His wife, his children, Rosie, her children, Lawrence far away—so many trusting people, such countless expectations, all in his hands. The question stymied him.

He returned of course, arriving at suppertime on Sunday night, to the delight at least of two-year-old Meghan. *"Andy!"* she shouted.

In Chicago the lilacs were out, the Sox in town. Loestroem put the garden in for Jo's parents. Here in Grand Forks traces of clotted snow remained in the woods. When the kids were settled he touched Rosie's shoulder as she stood over the sink. She looked pale and undernourished in her green sweatshirt.

"Did you make love to her?" Rosie asked. Her scalp was a blue gray along the part of her hair.

Loestroem didn't answer.

"I'm asking, did you make love?"

The bones of her shoulder felt foreign. She was scrubbing a black frying pan with a Brillo pad. "You did—I can tell," she said, scratching with the pad until the spot was scoured silver. "That's where I wish you'd be more like Larry. If you can't stand the truth, lie."

The Sioux Alumni beat the varsity in the spring football game. Untenured faculty members scrambled for positions. Loestroem's students were having trouble staying awake in his one o'clock class.

Rosie sat on a pink blanket, knees spread, rocking the stroller as the baby Erin nodded.

"Here's a nursery rhyme you don't recite in the Land of Lincoln," said
Rosie.

Hurray, Hurray, the first of May.
Screwing starts outside today.

Loestroem lay back on the lush grass, letting the sun fashion colors on
his eyelids. Life on the surface. The park, the city, the valley—all once
lay deep beneath the waters of Lake Agassiz. The receding of the lake
explained the flatness of the countryside. The ancient decaying life left
the soil fertile—the Bread Basket of the World. Things could be worse
than to live your life in the Bread Basket of the World. Order prevailed
here—a sense of predictability, as if the flatness kept the extremes of the
inhabitants in check.

Jeffie's Batman kite refused to take flight. He dragged it like a blanket
halfway across the field where students tossed Frisbees, and now one of
them took an interest in it.

Rosie watched, shading her eyes with her hand. "Andy?"

"Humm."

"Wanta do something crazy?"

Loestroem rolled over. "No. I still have the rash from last time."

He'd misread her tone. She waited for him to catch up. "This is crazier."

"How so?"

"When Larry gets here you go back and tell that woman everything."

Loestroem's mind came alive.

"You will anyway. People like you can't hold anything in." Then, to
soften it she added, "I mean, it would come out sooner or later anyway,
and then there's the blowup." She gave the stroller a little shove. "And
then it's over."

"Maybe."

"So why not preempt her? Do it quickly—one day of misery. Then
we'll meet, run away, me and you. You've considered it anyway, Andy,
and you know it."

That was one thing Loestroem disliked in Rosie, her belief that she could
read his thoughts.

Jeffie appeared with the repaired kite. Loestroem ran with the string,
puffing. It swooped upward, jerking Batman from side to side. The thing

needed more tail. A gust carried it toward the fence where it stuck. Rosie was tending to Meghan's unbuckled shoe strap. The kite string dug red grooves into Loestroem's fingers. "The kids?"

Rosie bit her lip. "Later maybe. I've done all I can for them. It's one more favor. The setting, me and Larry, it won't work."

Didn't she understand? He meant his own kids, too. "Where do we go?"

"L.A., San Diego. There's tons of teaching jobs in Southern California." Loestroem was afraid of California. "Not here?" he said.

"That's not running away."

"I don't know. How about somewhere closer to Chicago?"

"Okay, Chicago. Then we'll decide."

She was serious. He swallowed hard. *Escape.* Maybe he wasn't so mundane after all. The notion made him weak. Events were receding from him, growing distant, like the waters of Lake Agassiz. "Not *that* close. Minneapolis."

"Agreed. Minneapolis."

* * *

Bergantine. He remembers now. Prairieview Home, the directory says, without noting just where that is, as if we're born with certain knowledge. But Prairieview has its own listing so Loestroem phones, learns the location, and also that Miss April Bergantine is indeed in residence and pleased to entertain visitors for short periods.

April takes the sun in the corner of a rigidly maintained garden laden with hardy cactus-like plants, none of which are native to the Red River Valley. Her hair style hasn't changed and Loestroem finds that reassuring. A plastic tube coils from her nostrils to a valve on a narrow green cylinder on wheels. Beneath the rich henna hair a blanched face hangs, the jaw fixed.

Loestroem speaks first. "You probably don't recall me. We met back in the seventies."

"I recognized the walk. Andrew." She speaks in chopped sentences, pausing between phrases to gather breath. A tumbler of ice resting on her lap rattles with her jerky movements.

She arranges herself and they stroll, April pulling her oxygen tank. They speak of the dry weather, the new English Building, the composition of the reddish pebbles in the walkway. At last he mentions Rosie.

"Cancer," says April, mouthing the dread word with a fearless satisfaction, as if that's all that needs mentioning of Rosie's life.

"Yes. I only heard after I arrived here."

The face twists upward but says nothing.

This is arduous. "We didn't maintain communication," Loestroem says. He remembers how he looked to April as to an older sister, for approval.

April takes shallow breaths, like a basset hound. "Well, the bridge gang. Broke up, too, after." She lets Loestroem fill in the rest.

He wonders if she knows what became of Lem, and decides to spare her. The elderly have reason enough already to doubt human goodness. "I guess Larry going to Pullman ended those get-togethers."

April shakes her head. "Before that."

April could not be interested in such ancient tragedies. But she plunges ahead. "It was Rosie that quit the invitations. Fine with me."

Loestroem knows snatches of the story from Lem—how Larry got in late after a delay over a visa at LaGuardia, how the backup phone numbers Rosie wrote out for Jeffie didn't work. Everything went wrong. And then days later—as if to trump all the previous tricks—Larry announced he had no intention of rejoining his family.

Painful as it is, Loestroem wants to be filled in. "What did you hear?" He finds himself assuming April's speech pattern. "From this end?"

April's head twists sharply. "You don't know?"

Loestroem coughs into his hand. "I sort of withdrew. And I've wondered, with her gone."

"Bah, everyone's gone."

"Yes, so many years."

April's jaw goes slack as she thinks. "Larry got to the house—no Rosie." She pauses for breath. "The kids. Were there. Jeffie watching television. Meghan. Feeding oatmeal to the baby. Rosie vamoosed. And that's someone who called herself a mother."

The long sentence leaves April gasping, but Loestroem finds her choice of words comical. He interprets *vamoosed* as her signal that she's letting him off the hook. The familiar guilt over Rosie taking all the blame nicks his heart.

"County got involved. Endangerment. Relatives. Unitarians. But she ironed it out. Always good at that, Rosie. Ironing out."

That's one way of seeing it, Loestroem thinks. No one appreciates the agony for Rosie, the messages, the precautions, the frantic preparations — how with so few flights out of Grand Forks and Loestroem out of contact, it was get on the airplane or risk missing the moment forever.

They've circled back to April's corner near the tubular plants. The glass is sweating. No one hears of the northerly summer. Weathermen love to point to the dot on the map that is Grand Forks and cackle about the minus seventy wind-chill.

Loestroem is tiring of this stiff place and feels self-conscious in his ill-fitting jeans — the only visitor lacking a sport shirt and straw hat. He's never been at ease with the defect of illness.

April must want to know, what went wrong? Why, after all the fuss, did Rosie return as if from a weekend in the Twin Cities? She must believe Loestroem was involved, but in the way of things she probably remembers him for his style of bridge and capacity for beer. She asks no questions.

Loestroem says, "The strange thing is, in a different situation I think I could have become friends with Larry Tait. The little I knew him I liked him."

April snorts, recognizing the shallowness of the statement. But it was true, there was something good and reassuring about Larry. The way he sat contentedly with his cards while events and people swirled and flirted about him. He'd figured out who he was — he had no need to be noticed.

A small sandbag ashtray rests on the metal stand opposite the oxygen tank. April couldn't still be smoking. She draws a smashed pack of Marlboro Lights from her pocket. Her arm is tendon and bone. "Larry's not well at all. We're two of a kind."

Loestroem readies himself for more guilt. "I take it you kept in contact with Larry after he went west."

April's shoulders turn in her chair, stretching the tubing as she reaches. "Christmas cards. We visited once or twice. After he came back."

"Back here? To Grand Forks?"

April answers impatiently. "Yes. Then he had the stroke."

The building April directs him to is a red-brick condominium erected on what Loestroem remembers as a spacious field occupied in spring by pale undergraduates sprawled on colored towels. He knocks on 12-C and waits, uneasy, aware he's being examined through the tiny brass peephole. The old instinct—to run—nearly overtakes him, but he's come so far. A serious-faced tall man wearing rubber gloves answers the door, an attendant of some kind. His bushy eyebrows seem full of questions.

"Hello. I was given this address. I'm looking for a Mr. Tait."

A nod. "This is the home of Dr. Tait." The aroma of burned toast arises behind the man. From some distant corner come hollow, insincere daytime-television voices.

"Is this a good time to see him?"

The attendant appears amused. "He's had a spell." The eyebrows rise. There is something different about this man. "But if you'd be good enough to allow us a moment."

The cramped living-room with its three maroon sofas bears an elegant old-world stuffiness. The beveled mirror set above a teak captain's table is for some reason hanging low on the wall, offering Loestroem the unwelcome view of his own midsection. The top shelf of a handsome oak bookcase holds an armor helmet, breastplate, and a single gauntlet, all polished and dust free. This is far removed from the Tait household Loestroem once knew.

The attendant returns, properly dressed in a checked robe, and motions to Loestroem who follows through a sour-smelling carpeted hallway into what would be the master bedroom. Lawrence Tait sits in a wheelchair beside a screened window, his head turned toward a TV which is at the moment lifeless, though the remote switch rests close by on a desk. He is shriveled and hairless as an octopus.

"Hello Lawrence."

The head swivels. Loestroem sees a spark of recognition in the opaque corneas—but the spark is held too long. It must be anxiety. "Who?"

Aware of the attendant, Loestroem speaks slowly, in his classroom voice. "We met years ago. At the university. I'm Andy Loestroem."

Tait stares. "Who?"

The fright remains in his eyes and Loestroem has an idea. He forces himself to smile. Tait's face assumes a half-formed, toothy grin. The sour smell of the hall has given way to that of room deodorizer that is a combination of floral scents.

Still smiling, Loestroem says, "I was an instructor. Like you."

Tait looks at the attendant who shifts his feet, but his soft peeled face says nothing. Loestroem's smile muscles are tiring and his expression fades. No matter. Tait is losing interest. He slumps in the chair and turns his head. His neck has a boneless, scrubbed look.

"His mind skips," says the attendant. Tait seems little bothered that he's being talked about. With his good arm he reaches for the remote. Loestroem's attention is drawn to the huge dark desk with a ribbed rounded front where rest several small photographs in hardwood frames. Tait makes a tipping motion with his head and upper body, and the TV flickers to life. The clattering game show puts Loestroem enough at ease that he steps to the desk and studies the photos. They are all black-and-white posed shots of solemn men, one of whom in his bushy moustache and beret bears a striking resemblance to Lord Mountbatten.

The attendant speaks, as if to divert Loestroem. "Yes, we're not as fit as we once were."

Indeed, thinks Loestroem. April, Lem, Rosie. Disaster is making enquiries, tapping him on his shoulder.

Larry's pajamas are buttoned to the top but his robe has slid open, exposing a scaly abdomen and a twist of matted pubic hair. The sick know no embarrassment. "Does he receive physical therapy? Rehabilitation perhaps?"

The attendant flutters a hand before his face. "Oh, we had a beastly fracas over it. I'm quite capable, you see. I simply won't allow anyone else near him."

Then, as if his own mind has been unclogged, understanding forms. Loestroem stares at this attendant who, although younger, with his thin graying hair, soft neck and bleached skin is beginning to look like Lawrence Tait. "You may not recall my name since we never met. I was a close friend of Mrs. Tait."

Middleton raises an eyebrow slightly. "My word. *Professor* Loestroem."

"It happens that way with couples our age. They never stay with those they're having the affairs with. They build on it as a marriage-healer."

Loestroem believes that's the substance he offered Jo. Though at that moment he was supposed to be waiting in the lounge closest to the North-west counter at Minneapolis–St. Paul International Airport, he was instead encamped in a rented cabin on Lake Geneva.

He'd gone directly to Carbondale for the interview which was a disaster, and ended up drinking Pink Ladies with that Twain fanatic who dragged him over to Hannibal. So he lost a night and a day as well as his resistance. Naturally that was the one single time in her life that Jo (with Daddy's help) came up with a surprise—reserving the cabin, buying the food, packing the clothes.

Loestroem recalls these things as he sits low on an uncomfortable stone bench in the Commons near the Eternal Flame. Beautiful old Meredith Hall with its cinnamon brick and its tasteful murals of plump pioneer women in aprons, plows with wooden moldboards, and Red River ox carts has been given over to the Alumni Association. As at Madison, they care more about the departed. English has a new building, pretentious for English these days—massive gray with pillars all around and names carved into the balustrade:

dante * shakespeare * milton

Memories come to him of the sincere North Dakota students—their fear of failing, their eagerness to accept. He could have been happy here.

The confession did no good. He told it, he recalls, with the ending open: I'll do better—or, sorry but this is good-bye. It was interpreted by Jo as the first and the wall went up. His advice twenty years later is to lie. Rosie was right that he'd tell, and one thing more. He never did finish his dissertation.

A young woman descends the steps. She's seen fit to subject herself to one of those odd, half-shaved hair styles—as if she's saying two things at once. She's chewing gum. Loestroem recollects carrying a Ronson butane in a silver case for the convenience of beautiful girls who smoked cigarettes. This woman passes close to him and he smiles. She flicks a glance at him, processes the information, and does not return the smile. He feels old. This place, where once he was made welcome, has no use for him. There's nothing more to gain.

Yet that is not entirely true.

This time he knocks at the side entrance. As he waits he stares at the concrete step. The builder mixed fine gravel with the cement, creating an amalgamate. Twenty years ago Loestroem was as trapped as the sandstone pebbles in the step. Two cars glide by, one after another, tape decks thumping. The driver of the first drinks from a red can. *We're all such slobs.*

Jeffie looks him up and down, eases the door open. "I'm on my way to work."

Loestroem steps in. "I won't take long," he says, hoping his voice doesn't disclose his surprise that the kid actually works. The shades are pulled and it's cool inside. "Jeffie, can we talk about your mother?"

"It's *Jeff.* And she's dead."

As before, the words bite.

Jeff turns to the sink and draws a glass of water. *Carpetland,* it says on the back of his blue shirt. He drinks the water and motions to a wooden chair. "Honest, I got to be there in twenty minutes."

Jeff's life is exotic in its narrowness, living here in his old, safe home. Loestroem begins to grasp his strange connection to the young man. "Tell me," he says. "What was she like?"

Jeff sets the glass down and bites his upper lip, the way his mother used to, and Loestroem feels an upwelling of affection. "You said you knew her."

"For a short while. I need to know, was she—like, okay?"

Jeff smiles to himself at Loestroem's clumsy jargon. "She was super, we had no father."

"You mean—"

Jeff's voice takes on a hard edge. "I mean we never needed Lawrence Tait. Or you."

Loestroem should ignore the remark, but can't. "How's that?"

"Because Mom worked so hard."

"At a job?"

Jeffie—*Jeff* looks wounded. "She *ran* the admissions office."

Loestroem had expected to be overwhelmed with ghostly reminders, but it's not so. The kitchen is layered with personalities of people he doesn't know. The maple cabinets are painted over in a flat white, the knuckle-pinching handles replaced with routed wooden knobs. The floor which once contained linoleum patterned with marbly rectangles has been covered with a short-bristled blue-gray mat that runs six inches up the wall. Loestroem wishes he could lie down on this mat. "Did she go out much? See anybody?"

"Boyfriends?"

Loestroem swallows. "She was attractive."

"Sure, she got calls. You could tell. But like I say, she spent her time with us." Jeff's voice is softening. "We camped at Itasca first two weeks of every August, soon as Little League was over—Mom was my coach."

The comfort of a cool room and Jeff's warming manner work on Loestroem's emotions. He feels teary as he tells Jeff, "I loved your mother."

But this is not the right thing to say. Jeff turns toward the sink and runs another glass of water. "I knew about you. I hated you."

Loestroem wants to explain—he thinks he's good at alibis. But he invariably takes so long to formulate his response that others assume he has nothing to say—as when he sought to explain to the committee why he missed so many Monday classes, or when he explains to his children how busy he is. This time for once, he shuts up.

Jeff says, "You and Lawrence Tait." He tries to banter. "Doesn't say much for English Lit teachers, does it?"

This ingrate knows nothing. All the reasons he has to hate and he's got it wrong. No one's yet told him that his mother tried to abandon him. "You and your father didn't connect when he came back then."

Jeff's eyes narrow. "We called. The butler would answer."

"Middleton?"

"That's what we called him, the butler. Look, I was a sophomore when he came back and it was only a year till he had the stroke. There was mix-ups like I can't even tell you."

They've talked now for twenty minutes. Jeff has not moved from the sink. The chair is awkward, but Loestroem is close to something. "Why did she not want me to know about her death?"

Jeff sighs. "I maybe gave you the wrong idea. She didn't want people to know she was sick. She made me knock when I went to her bedroom so she could get her wig on."

They are silent for a moment. Grieving together, Loestroem believes. He checks the clock above the sink. "I'm keeping you."

Jeff shrugs. "It's okay."

"Did she ever talk about me?"

Jeff bites his upper lip. "Quite a bit the last year. Some before." He pauses for a deep breath. "I don't know. More than Lawrence Tait."

This surprises Loestroem. "I guess the thing with Middleton made it clumsy."

"*No!* That *wasn't* it." Jeff's voice is dry. "It's because . . ." His eyes tear over.

Loestroem suppresses the urge to wrap his arms around Rosie's son. "Tell me, Jeff."

"She said *you* were my father."

Loestroem says one word. "Me?"

"She said, when we were little and we always believed it, that this super guy, not Tait, was our real dad. She said some day, and she was sure of this, he'd come back and we'd be a family. You'd make us laugh, the way you sing, and take us to air shows, and make homemade kites, and you'd teach me to swing left-handed."

As little as he knows of such things, Loestroem is pleased.

Jeff wipes his eyes. "It kept Meghan going."

"Meghan, yes. Where is she?"

"Still at Smith, getting her doctorate."

Loestroem can't form the picture. He thinks of the envelopes his daughter sends, stuffed with photos of her children, as if to compensate for the lack of words that are fields of quicksand they choose to leave untrod.

"What was taking me so long, supposedly?"

"You were working it out, Mom said. We believed. It was just a fact, like you know Disneyworld is there even if you've never seen it? Mom was great at telling stories."

Jeff rips a square from a roll of paper towel and blows his nose. "I got to know Wisconsin plates. I'm so stupid. When you pulled up the other day I thought, Well—he *finally* made it. I knew it was you—Mom said you walked funny. But I got afraid."

Loestroem thinks, *Considering all the troubles I've carried through this door you do well to be afraid.*

"She never said she didn't want you to know. Everything was so far gone by then. I was confused. I didn't know what to do. I still don't."

Even Loestroem has caught on that the secret to overcoming confusion is to keep going. If it looks like you're competent no one questions you. You prepare your 101 lectures by reading a chapter ahead, three times a week, Monday, Wednesday, Friday. You stop at Piggly Wiggly, stroll the open cases of cellophane packages knowing something will present itself for dinner. While there you're reminded that you need cereal and milk. Nowhere does anyone ask if you've written your mother and are faithful to your wife. Soon a week is gone, the semester has passed, and nothing tragic has happened.

This is the advice he'd give to Jeff. But as an adult Jeff has likely already received a glut of advice and rejected it all. "When you understood the truth, it was okay?"

Jeff wipes his eyes. "She never told until she found out the cancer was in her pancreas. What could I say then – everybody should get to die happy, don't you think?"

He nods. Does Jeff include his father? Loestroem has sense enough not to ask. "Especially your mother."

At last Loestroem stands, looking around as Jeff composes himself. "Say, is that what they call a digital synthesizer?"

"By the table? Yeah, that's my Sansui."

"I think my son has one of those. In fact I know he does."

Jeff looks at him, mouth open. "Your real son?"

"Yes, and there's a real daughter, too."

Jeff is shaking his head. "Weird. A brother and sister I don't even know."

Jo shook sand from Lizzie's bathing suit. Loestroem sat on the dock, his feet in the water. Out on the lake gulls swept low over two big-shouldered men trolling in a green and white boat, their rods angling toward the cloudless sky.

Loestroem tortured himself imagining the scene of Rosie waiting in the Minneapolis airport. She'd have dressed in something other than her sweatshirt, resolving the dilemma of what to wear when you abandon your family by donning a ruffled blouse and light brown slacks with a flare at the ankles. She'd go from counter to counter, asking for messages. She'd meet all the flights from all the possible places Loestroem might fly in from – St. Louis, Springfield, Milwaukee. Frustrated that they hadn't come up with a contingency plan, yet ready to laugh at the misunderstanding (Thank God – I was worried to death you'd changed your mind!), she'd neglect to eat and avoid sleep. The second day she'd buy coffee and an airport cookie from the fifteen dollars she carried in her purse.

By the end of the same day Loestroem was in physical pain, his skull splitting, his body heavy and lifeless from guilt. He half expected Rosie to show up at the cabin, descending the stone steps dug into the hillside, dragging her suitcases. He was cramped and sore from sitting in the wooden deck chair, and exhausted from indecision. His family caught on at once that this wasn't the man who left, that some fearsome burden had attached itself to him. The kids managed their childish adjustment, making do for once with each other as playmates, while Jo stayed in the cabin, taming her own fears, or sat in the other deck chair, *Family Circle* folded open on her lap.

In Minneapolis airliners arrived and landed, big heavier-than-air machines painted in bright, stylized swooping letters, designed to reassure the wary. The uniformed agents began to recognize her—a good-looking woman working hard at keeping her poise.

"Anything for me—Tait with an I?"

"Afraid not."

"How about Loestroem?"

"Sorry."

"Try Willet."

"Nothing yet."

That evening she gave in and used the phone to try Loestroem's in-laws. It rang ten, fifteen times as she listened, squeezing the cord. An old woman, hard of hearing, answered. Who? No, he was in Wisconsin. Wisconsin. Oh yes, he got back from Dakota. Well, she wasn't real sure now, at a lake, she thought. Who is this? Who? No, no idea.

The third day, about the hour Rosie, worn down and humiliated, was calling Larry and then her father collect to ask for money for a ticket back, Loestroem burst forth with his confession. He left much out, smoothed over hurtful parts, and made no mention of present plans. "A situation happened to me," was the way he began.

What Jo wanted to know was how soon after he got there had he started seeing this person. Loestroem knew that by "seeing" she meant "sleeping with." After it was over, with stunning grace, Jo walked back inside, her hand on her cheek, taking care not to trip on the uneven ground fronting the cabin, and changed out of her swim suit into her traveling clothes. Thereafter, shared days would be filled with stretches of poisonous silence interrupted by storms of questions arising from somewhere within the impenetrable fortress of Jo, the kids, her parents. "What you've done isn't right," said Jo, little knowing.

Sitting on the dock, Loestroem felt no better for his efforts. The curious thing was that he and Rosie never resolved where they'd go. Getting away seemed all that counted.

When Loestroem was fifteen his father after exiting Kroger's with an *Argosy* and a number two can of fruit cocktail lurched against a wooden telephone pole and fell dead of a heart attack. The boy went to sleep that evening knowing that Bud Loestroem who oiled his hair and owned only black lace shoes had died, but each time he awoke he found he had to relearn what had happened, still trying to fit the fact to a place of permanence in his mind. For months he got up for the bathroom saying to himself, "Remember, Dad died."

The minnows tickled his toes, nibbling. Loestroem watched the silent fishermen. The man in the stern heaved to his left, rippling the water. Loestroem imagined himself plunging past the fishermen as from a point in the sky, feet first the way he used to drop from the rusting cables beneath the old Highway 29 bridge, pinching his nostrils and trying to point his toes downward. But instead of striking the fine-grained ooze of the Sangamon, here he'd keep going, falling away from his tangled life, air bubbling upward through the eternally yielding water, the colors changing—azure, indigo, black; his plunging feet sensing the temperature gradient—warm, cooler, chill. Either way, whichever way, he knew now he'd be a long time getting back to the surface.

GARY ELLER grew up in North Dakota, lived in Alaska where he worked as a pharmacist, and began writing seriously when to his astonishment, he realized he'd become middle-aged. Eller studied at the Iowa Writer's Workshop, graduating in 1989. His fiction has appeared in several publications, and he is the winner of the 1993 River City Short Fiction Award. Eller is nearing completion on a long novel set in Alaska. He lives in Ames, Iowa, with his wife, Marianne Malinowski, and their black cats.